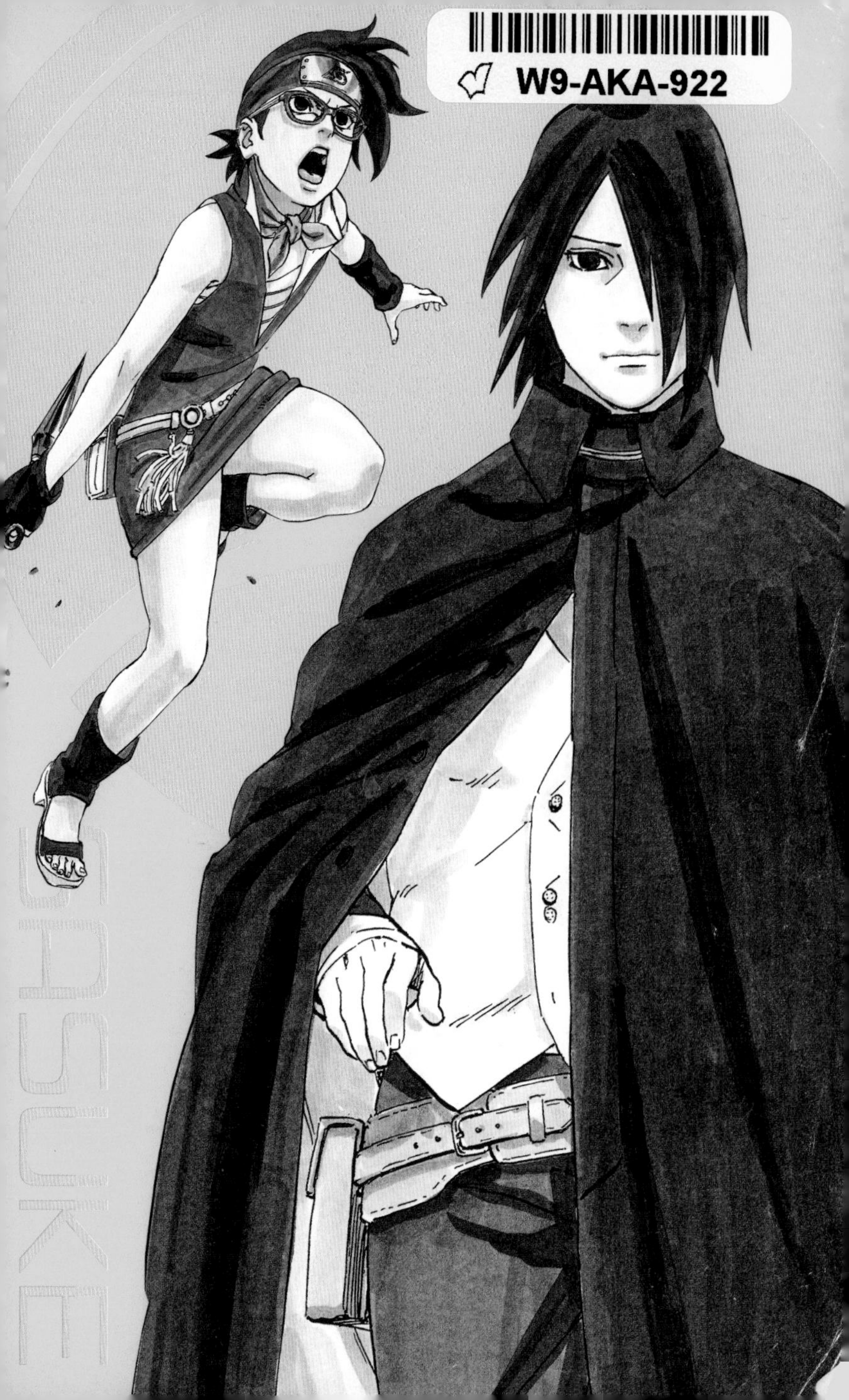

SASUKE'S STORY

STAR PUPIL

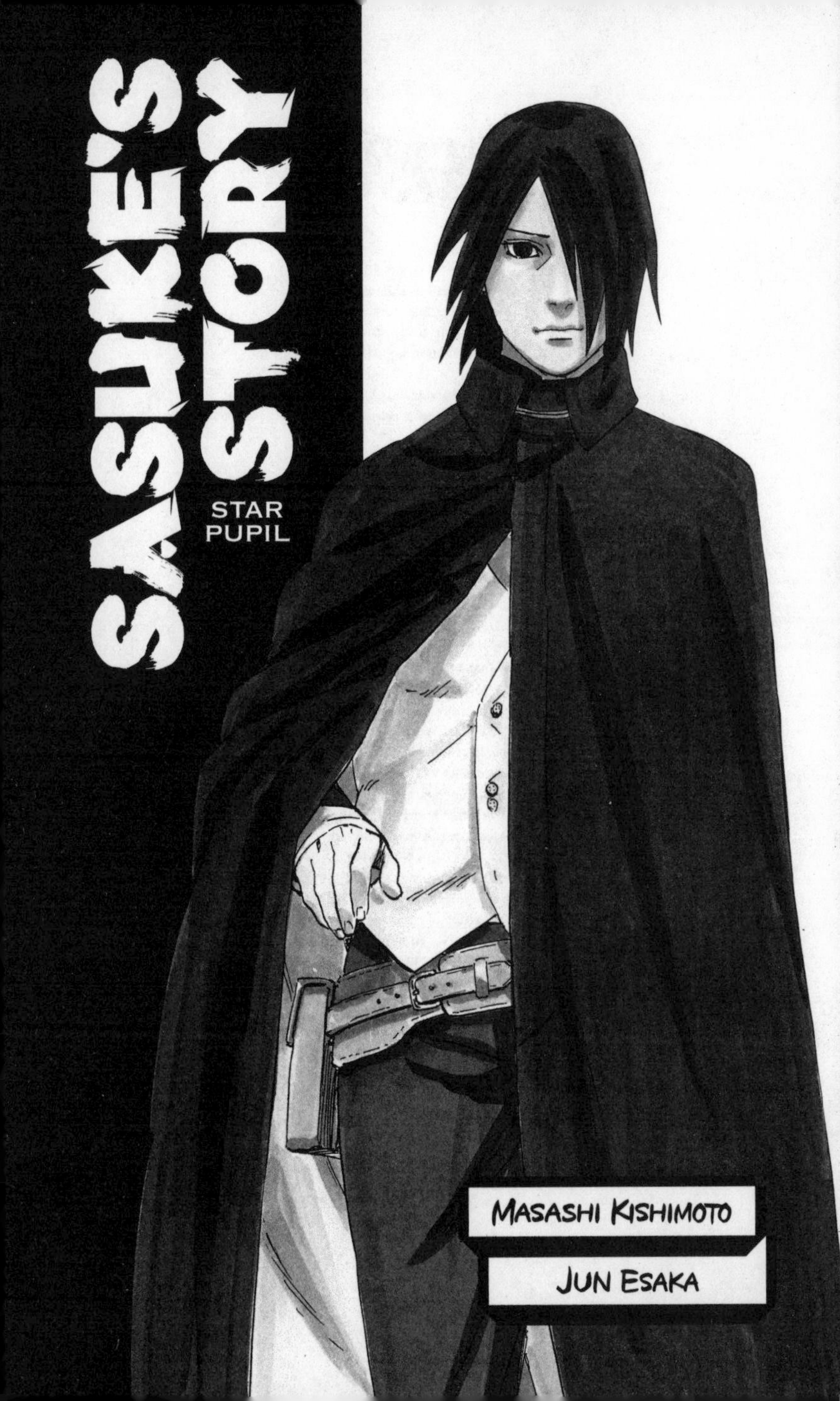

Masashi Kishimoto

Jun Esaka

NARUTO SASUKE-SHINDEN
© 2018 by Masashi Kishimoto, Jun Esaka
All rights reserved.
First published in Japan in 2018 by SHUEISHA Inc., Tokyo.
English translation rights arranged by SHUEISHA Inc.

COVER + INTERIOR DESIGN Shawn Carrico
TRANSLATION Jocelyne Allen

Published by VIZ Media, LLC
P.O. Box 77010
San Francisco, CA 94107

Library of Congress Cataloging-in-Publication Data

Names: Esaka, Jun, author. | Kishimoto, Masashi, 1974- author. | Allen,
Jocelyne, 1974- translator.
Title: Sasuke shinden--star pupil / [original story by] Masashi Kishimoto ;
[adapted by] Jun Esaka ; translation by Jocelyne Allen.
Other titles: Sasuke shinden, shitei no hoshi. English
Description: San Francisco, CA : VIZ Media, LLC, [2020] | Series: Naruto |
Audience: Grades 10-12 | Summary: "When Sasuke is given the task of
training of Team Seven, Boruto is delighted, but he has trouble
accepting his master's teachings. And then pop star Himeno Lily jumps in
with a mission for them."-- Provided by publisher.
Identifiers: LCCN 2020010292 (print) | LCCN 2020010293 (ebook) | ISBN
9781974713325 (trade paperback) | ISBN 9781974718559 (ebook)
Subjects: CYAC: Ninja--Fiction. | Teacher-student relationships--Fiction.
Classification: LCC PZ7.1.E816 Sas 2020 (print) | LCC PZ7.1.E816 (ebook)
| DDC [Fic]--dc23
LC record available at https://lccn.loc.gov/2020010292
LC ebook record available at https://lccn.loc.gov/2020010293

Printed in the U.S.A.
First Printing, October 2020

VIZ MEDIA

viz.com

SHONEN
JUMP

CONTENTS

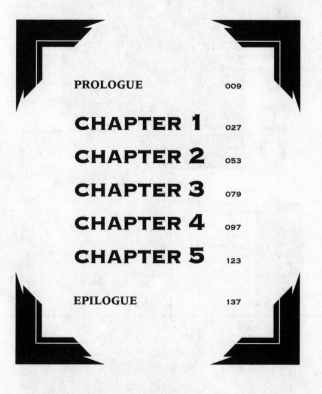

CHARACTERS

UCHIHA SASUKE

Naruto's rival and friend. Sarada's father. Master to Boruto's student.

UZUMAKI NARUTO

The Seventh Hokage, Boruto's father. The hero who saved Konohagakure.

UCHIHA SARADA

Konohagakure Genin. Sasuke is her father. Team Seven member with Boruto.

UZUMAKI BORUTO

Konohagakure Genin. Naruto is his father, Sasuke is his master.

SARUTOBI KONOHAMARU

Konohagakure Jonin. He leads Team Seven. The Third Hokage was his father.

MITSUKI

Konohagakure Genin. Orochimaru is his father. Team Seven member with Boruto.

PROLOGUE

SASUKE'S STORY: STAR PUPIL

PROLOGUE

The Thunder Rail train chugged along, its squat smokestack spitting out a trail of white. Sarutobi Konohamaru leaned back in his seat and stared absently at the world of green and brown sliding past outside. The tracks seemed endless, meandering this way and that, stitching the valley together. The scene outside the window—an expanse of lush, green trees, occasionally broken by the white and pink of dogwoods in bloom—showed no sign of changing any time soon.

Konohamaru let his mind wander. He thought about what he'd have for supper. *I gotta grab something to eat when I get back. Maybe Ichiraku Ramen? Although I should actually whip something up myself and save money for once...* Although he was always hammering into Boruto and the other genin the importance of never letting one's guard down no matter what the mission, he was not particularly concerned with watching his back when he was on the road home from a solo errand-boy mission with essentially zero chance of battle.

Wish this thing would hurry up...

Yawning, Konohamaru stretched his arms out. He noticed a certain person sitting up ahead, and he froze in place. A man with hair hanging across half of his face and his black cloak hiding the rest—Uchiha Sasuke. He appeared to be sleeping.

Weird that Sasuke's here. I guess he's making a report.

Konohamaru stared with great interest at the sleeping Sasuke. Famously handsome since boyhood, his face showed no sign of decline even now. His faintly visible crow's feet only added an air of sophistication to his sharp features. A pair of special eyes hid behind those closed lids—the Sharingan and Rinnegan.

One of the most powerful ninja in the world, not to mention extremely cool and unbelievably handsome to boot, he had made any number of women swoon when he was single. Whether or not he himself had been the slightest bit interested in any of that was another matter, however.

Can't believe I'd run into Sasuke here.

Konohamaru looked around the carriage once more. An infant fast asleep on its mother's lap, an elderly couple splitting a dorayaki cake, a younger man and woman on their way home from a trip. The people who shared this car with him were villagers who rejoiced in the current peace, entirely removed from the bloody world of the shinobi. Konohamaru had to admit that Sasuke's ability to fall asleep in the midst of such a group was an impressive feat.

It was hard to get a handle on what exactly Sasuke's position was in the village of Konohagakure. He was so famous that he was a super-rare card in the Extreme Ninja game, but he also rarely showed his face in the village, and officially, he was a criminal on probation. He had just as many enemies as allies. If the other passengers were to realize they were sharing a car with *the* Uchiha Sasuke, there would inevitably be a commotion, but not a soul noticed him.

Konohamaru closed his eyes, thinking about napping himself. He pressed his head up against the window and got comfortable in his seat.

Boom!

An explosion rocked the carriage. His eyes flew open in surprise. Konohamaru looked out the window to see flames and black smoke pouring from the caboose.

"An explosion!" shrieked a passenger. "Smoke!"

Instantly, panic enveloped the carriage.

"No! I don't want to die!"

"Stop! Don't push!"

"Run! To the front of the train! Hurry!"

Jostling up against one another, the passengers flooded the narrow aisle.

"Please, calm down!" Konohamaru called out, stepping into the fray. The mass hysteria could cause more damage than the explosion itself. "I'm a ninja from the Land of Fire! The explosion was in the last car! Very far from us! Everyone, please calm down and...stay in your own seat for now! Quietly!"

Silence immediately fell over the carriage. Some measure of order had been restored thanks to Konohamaru's direction. He hesitated over whether or not to lead them to the front of the train. If the explosion was the doing of some villain, then the lead carriage would be a definite target, given that that was where all the controls were.

"I'm going to go take a look at the situation. I'm sure the train will stop soon. Once it does, please exit the carriage, taking the bare minimum of luggage with you. And whatever you do, don't panic, please!"

Where's Sasuke? He looked around, but the other ninja was gone, presumably having already headed out to the site of the explosion. It seemed he had prioritized putting out the fire over calming the passengers.

Konohamaru hurried to open the window and climbed up to the roof of the car before racing to the caboose, ground zero for the explosion.

✖ ✖ ✖ ✖ ✖

Arriving at the twelfth car, the tail of the train, Konohamaru stopped dead in his tracks, stunned. The car should have been entirely ablaze, and yet for some reason it and the bright flames enveloping it were frozen solid. He kicked in one of the icy windows and climbed inside. A biting wind blasted past, almost sharp enough to cut his cheek.

Uchiha Sasuke stood in the center of a vortex of cold air. The red fire that burned up the wooden seat frame before his brandished hand was suddenly encased in ice. An instant later, it disappeared.

"Sasuke? What on earth…?"

"Konohamaru?" Sasuke turned and flicked his eyes around the frozen carriage. "As you can see, I extinguished the fire."

"E-extinguished… Well, it's true the fire's out, but…"

The last car was for first-class passengers, so the design was different from the other carriages. Pairs of luxuriously large sofas faced each other, and thick oak walls separated the compartments. The explosion had devastated the ceiling, but it didn't take an expert to see that the light fixtures and ceiling fans were quite sumptuous, even if the intricate sculptures that had adorned them were now in pieces on the floor. The blast had also warped all the furniture in the car. Now the seats were frozen as well as charred, a sad shadow of their former glory.

"Putting out fires with Water Style generates high-temperature steam," Sasuke told an overwhelmed Konohamaru. "So just combine Water with Wind Style and freeze everything, including the steam you generate."

"A sort of Ice Style that's not Water, hm?"

"Close, but not exactly." Sasuke shook his head. "A long time ago, I fought someone who used this technique. I copied it, but my approximation doesn't begin to compare with the power of his original."

It doesn't begin to compare? This?

A puff of white air slipped from his lips as Konohamaru examined the carriage, completely frozen floor to ceiling. It was one thing to say you "just" had to combine Water Style with Wind Style, but it was no mean feat to activate these two different natures simultaneously and somehow bring them together.

"Eeah!"

Konohamaru turned at this brief cry from the doorway.

"W-w-what is this...?" A teenage girl with short red hair stood there gaping, earrings dangling from her ears, nails decorated with rhinestones and glitter. "Why is my seat frozen solid?"

"There was an explosion in this car," Konohamaru explained. "We had to put the fire out."

"An explosion?!" The girl's eyes nearly popped out of her head. "When?!"

"Just a minute ago," he replied, perplexed. "You were here and you didn't notice?"

"I thought everyone was being weird, all running and yelling. I was listening to music." And indeed, orange headphones hung around her neck.

Sasuke took a step forward "What were you doing up to now?" he asked, his voice flat.

"What was I...? I was kinda hungry, so I had, um, pasta and escargot and panna cotta in the dining car. And then I got some water to bring back here with me." The girl held up the glass of carbonated water she held in one hand as if to show it off.

"What happened to the other passengers?" Sasuke asked.

"It's just me. I mean, this is first class. I rented the whole carriage!" She puffed her chest out with self-satisfaction.

Konohamaru stared hard. This girl? All alone in first class?

"What's that look for?" She pursed her lips and frowned at the suspicious look on Konohamaru's face. "Are underage people not allowed to ride the Thunder Train alone?"

"No, that's not—"

"Don't get the wrong idea, buddy. I've got money! Maybe I look like—"

Sasuke cut the girl off. "Konohamaru. Did you notice anyone suspicious on your way here?"

"No." Konohamaru shook his head. "I came here on the roof, though, so I don't know what's going on inside the train."

"The person who planted the bomb must still be on board." Sasuke tossed Konohamaru a fragment of glass.

The thin shard had a gentle curve to it, clearly different from the window glass. Konohamaru realized it was part of a bomb timer fuse. If the perpetrator had employed a bomb to cause the explosion, then it was safe to assume the crime was the work of someone who couldn't use ninjutsu. And if they couldn't use ninjutsu, there was no way they could escape the Thunder Train when it was racing along like a bolt of lightning across the ground. In other words, the bomber was still on the train. He and Sasuke needed to apprehend whoever it was before they could do any more damage.

Boom!

The roar of another explosion.

"This one's at the head of the train!" he shouted, peering out the window.

"The train's speeding up." Sasuke took in the scene outside before nimbly using the window frame as a foothold and clambering up to the top of the car.

"S-Sasuke?!" Konohamaru yelped.

The other ninja tore across the roof to the lead car in the blink of an eye. Without so much as a pause to catch his breath, he leaped into the billowing smoke.

Calm down, Konohamaru told himself. It was important to work together, especially in emergency situations.

The fact that the train was speeding up after the second bomb meant that the control panel had likely been destroyed. And if that were the case, then the only way to immediately and safely bring the train to a halt was to stop the actual moving parts of the vehicle. Sasuke's ice technique would do the job nicely. If Sasuke was off to stop the train, then Konohamaru should focus on catching the bomber inside.

It took him about two seconds to reach this conclusion. Getting to work with a top-rate ninja like Sasuke was an extremely valuable experience, but the scope of his own jutsu and the speed of his judgement were on an entirely different level. It was a bit of work just to keep up.

At any rate, I have to secure the bomber inside the train. Konohamaru was about to leave the carriage when he suddenly remembered something and turned around.

The girl from first class was tapping the ice wall curiously.

"Please don't leave this car," he told her. "It's dangerous."

"Okay!" the girl languidly replied, snapping an icicle off the frozen wall to use in place of a stir stick in her fizzy water.

Is she going to be okay here? Aah, but I don't have the time to stay with her. With a feeling of hazy apprehension, Konohamaru stepped into the eleventh car.

✖ ✖ ✖ ✖ ✖

The second-class seats were deserted, the chairs and aisle

strewn with bags and passenger detritus. The passengers themselves had likely evacuated to the front. This was only natural, given that the explosion had happened in the car directly behind them.

Konohamaru passed cautiously through this wasteland to enter the tenth car. Its passengers had also fled, leaving another empty carriage—or so he thought until he came across a woman curled up in the corner of a seat, her back shaking.

"Um, are you all right?" Konohamaru asked.

The woman jumped in surprise and turned. Her face was a mess of tears, and she held a baby up to her chest. She'd apparently been too frightened to move.

"Wh-who are you?" she gasped.

"A ninja from the village of Konohagakure. No need to be afraid now. We put out the fire from the explosion."

"Oh, thank goodness." She breathed a sigh of relief. "So my baby and I are safe, then?"

"Yes. Please stay calm and remain in your seat," Konohamaru instructed.

He started past her.

"Wait!" the woman called out to stop him. "Please. I'm begging you. Don't leave me alone. I'm scared. I'm so scared."

"Okay, um, just calm down," he said. *I don't have time for this. I need to find that bomber.* With some annoyance, Konohamaru turned back.

The woman flung her baby at him.

"Your baby!" He instinctively reached out to catch it, but by the time the he realized what was actually happening, it was already too late.

With a *fump*, the baby turned into a ninja in a deep-purple costume and thrust a kunai toward Konohamaru. He threw his head backward, but the blade still scraped his cheek. Blood poured down the side of his face.

The baby's a ninja transformation! So then is the mother an accomplice?

The thought had no sooner formed in his mind than he felt a foot slam into his back. At some point, the helpless mother had also transformed into a ninja, and now she came flying at him with a right uppercut aimed squarely at his side.

"Pretty nasty trick to pretend to be weak to get my guard down!" He kicked hard at the ceiling to send his body in the opposite direction and evade the not-a-mother's fist. But he wasn't going to be able to dodge the other one's kunai closing in on his left. He caught it with his wrist covering and absorbed the force of the blow, then turned around to strike the ninja with a backhand to the face.

He saw something glimmer in the corner of his eye— shuriken! He jumped back down the aisle as far as he could to get some distance and faced the two ninja once again.

One, a man past middle age, still had a bib tied around his neck, a vestige of his baby transformation. A cloth covered the other one's face, but judging from his build, Konohamaru assumed he was a man as well. The sole distinguishing feature he could make out was a mole beneath the left eye. Both had weapons at the ready.

"So you are a jonin, judging from the way you carry yourself," the man with the bib said.

"Hmm, dunno." Konohamaru wasn't about to give his enemy any information. "All us Konoha ninja are pretty strong. Maybe I'm not even a chunin yet."

"You're too modest." The man in the bib shook his head. "I am grateful to the fates."

"Huh?"

"I never dreamed I would be given the opportunity to kill a jonin with my own hands."

All right, tough guy. Konohamaru glanced out the window.

Their speed was dropping, albeit by the tiniest increments. Sasuke had probably frozen the mechanical parts at the head of the train. *I gotta take care of this before he gets back, give him a little present.*

"There's no need for you to fight." The man with the mole took a step out in front of the man with the bib. "We will dispatch him."

"We?" Konohamaru raised an eyebrow.

The door leading to the ninth car opened behind the mole-faced man, and a new purple shadow strolled in.

"So there's more of you!" Konohamaru jumped back again. *Three against one.*

Before this had a chance to register fully, a fourth purple-clad ninja appeared behind the third, then another behind him, and still another behind that one.

Four, five, six...

Twelve against one.

This was no time to worry about taking them alive. As the twelve ninja closed in on him, Konohamaru backed away until he bumped up against the door and was forced to stop.

No, no, hang on a sec. This many people are gonna fight in this tiny train car?

"Whoa, time o—"

Twelve ninja slashed toward him from three different directions. There was nowhere for him to run in the claustrophobic space. So then Shadow Doppelganger—Wait, no, a melee in this small room was too dangerous.

Gah! For real! What am I gonna do here?!

For the moment, he focused on dodging their kunai. A powerful gust of hot wind blasted past him, nearly singing the top of his head—Fire Style: Fireball Technique. The enemy ninja flinched and retreated, forced back by the sudden eruption of crimson flames.

"Uchiha Sasuke!" the mole-faced man groaned as he beat back the roaring flames.

Sasuke stood over Konohamaru, still crouched on the floor. "Situation?" he asked.

"This is probably the entire enemy contingent on the train. Leader's the old guy in the bib. Very likely they've got a larger organization backing them."

"Take them alive," Sasuke instructed.

"Right," Konohamaru said, and the other ninja vanished.

Konohamaru looked up and gasped. The man in purple at the far end of the enemy line was already frozen and falling to the floor. The man next to him also dropped to his knees and toppled over. In the blink of an eye, Sasuke had taken down two ninja.

"Leave him to us!" A man jumped in front of the one in the bib to protect him.

Without a word, Sasuke thrust his still-sheathed hidden sword downward. The man caught the sword stroke with his wrist covering, but there was no way it could absorb the blow completely, and the man flew back against the wall.

After a moment's hesitation, the bibbed man charged toward the window, broke the glass, and leaped outside.

"Ah! Hey! Stop!" Konohamaru glanced at Sasuke, but he didn't seem to be paying any mind to the man in the bib.

Which means I'm supposed to go after him?

Konohamaru jumped through the window to give chase.

✖ ✖ ✖ ✖ ✖

Alternating between hand strikes and the back of his sword, Sasuke knocked his enemies out cold one after another. Even just in terms of speed, he was on an entirely different level than his opponents. They had no chance, despite outnumbering him, and they dropped like flies.

Soon only two of the purple-clad men remained standing. One of them was the man with the mole who had transformed into the mother. Sasuke stared at him, silently willing him to surrender.

"Dammit." The mole-faced man sighed and waved a short sign. *Pok!*

A horn-shaped steel pillar sprang up from the floor at Sasuke's feet. He deftly stepped out of its path and punched the man closest to him in the jaw, knocking him out. The pillar continued to grow. It ripped through the ceiling of the car and twisted upward into the sky. Sasuke had never seen this ninjutsu before, and while it appeared quite powerful, it was still no match for him. At any rate, there was just one enemy ninja left now.

Sasuke looked squarely at the last man standing, the man with the mole.

"Hngh! Come, Uchiha!" The mole-faced man desperately yanked his sword from the sheath on his back and readied it before him.

"Hey? Is the train, like, stopped?" a voice drawled lazily.

The door opened behind the mole-faced man, and the girl from the first-class car popped her head in.

"Run!" Sasuke shouted.

But mole-faced man was already rushing at the girl to grab her.

"Huh?" She raised both eyebrows, confused by the sudden attack.

Sasuke flung a kunai with unerring precision. It pierced the mole-faced man's stomach but didn't stop him. He yanked the girl off her feet and tossed her toward the window. She screamed. The glass broke, and she was launched from the train.

"Tch!" Sasuke leaped after her, caught her in midair, and touched down on the ground.

"W-w-what?! That was super scary! Who was that guy?! I totes thought I was gonna die!"

If she was making this much of a fuss, then she couldn't be badly hurt. The bigger problem was the mole-faced man.

Sasuke let the girl down on a patch of grass and turned back toward the train. He jumped up, caught the edge of a window frame, and peered inside.

The inside of the carriage was painted with blood, and the mole-faced man lay slumped against the wall. His feet continued to twitch, but his wide-open eyes stared blankly at nothing. It was clear he was dead. He looked to have slit his own throat with the kunai on the floor in front of him.

This is exactly what I didn't want.

Sasuke flipped over the other man who was face down on the floor. Blood oozed from his chest where a kunai had been stabbed into him. The man with the mole had probably killed him to keep him quiet.

Sasuke sighed with annoyance. Train bombers or not, he hadn't intended for anyone to die. Now he would never get any information about why they'd committed this crime, and besides, the current Hokage hated it when people died. If Konohamaru could at least take the leader alive…

Sasuke turned his back on the eleven dead bodies and jumped down out of the train.

The girl was on her back on the ground, her eyes dazed. She was trembling uncontrollably.

"What's wrong?" Sasuke asked.

"Ah…ah…" Her voice shook. She raised an unsteady hand.

As he looked back in the direction of her pointing finger, Sasuke understood that his last hope had been crushed already.

The steel column the mole-faced man had created with his ninjutsu had risen up from the ground, twisted through the passenger seats, pierced the roof, and stretched sharply up to the heavens. Skewered on the tip was the man who had been their leader, impaled like a butcher bird's prey on a twig.

✖ ✖ ✖ ✖ ✖

"Hold up!" Konohamaru called out to the fleeing man in the bib. "You're not gonna make it out of here! Just surrender!"

The man ignored him and ran toward the woods that spread out on the side of the tracks.

Konohamaru turned the knob on the scientific ninja tool attached to the inside of his wrist. A small scroll popped out. In it was an electrical strike that used Thunder Style.

He released the bolt from the palm of his brandished hand. Crackling and sparking, it raced off into space like a yellow dragon and struck the man in the bib squarely in the back. The man pitched forward, his body shuddering, but a moment later he picked himself back up and took off running as though nothing had happened.

Huh? Misfire?

The scientific ninja team had calibrated the lightning bolt to paralyze without killing. It had definitely hit its target. Was the man in the bib resistant to electricity?

Konohamaru scrambled up on top of the train and launched a sickle and chain. The weight attached to the tip of the sickle caught the bibbed man's feet.

First, let's bring this fight to close quarters!

He yanked on the sickle, and the man's body flew up into space. The man carved an arc in the air as he was pulled in, building momentum to swing his fist at Konohamaru's face. Konohamaru blocked with his left hand and grabbed the man's head. He threw his own head forward in a head butt, fully prepared to crack his own head open if necessary.

Whud!

The sound and the impact rattled his skull. Ignoring the pain in his eardrums, Konohamaru quickly kneaded his chakra.

Rasen…

The man ripped off the bib. With the square of fabric clenched in his hand, he grabbed hold of Konohamaru's foot. Konohamaru felt something small and hard embedded in the fabric press against his ankle.

Dammit! He started to twist his ankle away.

The bib exploded.

Intense pain raced up his right leg. He'd manage to avoid a direct hit, but fragments of the bomb nevertheless punched deep into his calf, the shards digging into his flesh before finally falling around him.

The man's right hand had been cleanly blown off by the blast. He swung at Konohamaru's face with this mangled arm. Spraying blood landed in Konohamaru's eyes. "Ngh!" Unbearable pain shot through him, but he kept his eyes open through sheer force of will.

He grabbed and twisted the man's arm upward "What do you want? Why are you targeting this train?!"

"Want?" The man stared back. "To kill you, ninja of Konoha!" He kicked out at Konohamaru.

With his leg injured, Konohamaru couldn't maintain his balance, but the reactive force of the blow caused the man himself to stagger backward as well.

Now! Konohamaru focused his chakra in his palm. This time for sure, Rasen—

A dark steel pillar erupted from the roof of the train, stabbing into the bibbed man. "Gah!" He vomited blood as his suddenly splayed legs twitched and spasmed, kicking at empty space.

Dragging his leg behind him, Konohamaru ran-walked to examine the man's face.

His eyes bulged, and his cheeks were drawn taut. His tongue lolled from his mouth, a stream of blood dribbling from it. A drop fell onto Konohamaru's shoe. The man was dead.

"Dammit..." Konohamaru slowly collapsed on the spot. He pulled out one of the metal fragments stabbing into his calf. How could he face Sasuke now? Not only had he not managed to get any information, he'd let the enemy die.

CHAPTER 1

SASUKE'S STORY: STAR PUPIL

"Master Konohamaru! We came to visit ya!"

The door to his hospital room flew open. The first to come careening in was Uzumaki Boruto. He arrived empty-handed, despite the custom of bringing flowers or a gift to an injured teacher in the hospital.

"Boruto! You're too loud! This is a hospital! Quiet!" Uchiha Sarada chided her teammate as she followed him into the room, holding a bouquet of sakura blossoms to her chest.

"How are you feeling, Master Konohamaru?" Mitsuki was the last to enter, carrying a paper bag and looking relaxed as ever.

It was only his first day in the hospital, but Konohamaru was bored senseless already. He very nearly—carelessly—smiled at the arrival of his beloved students, but managed to suppress the grin at the last second.

"Whoa, whoa," he said coolly, careful to maintain his strict demeanor before his pupils. "What happened to your mission?"

"No missions today! So we were up bright and early making it happen!"

"Happen?"

"He means this." Mitsuki pulled a square package out of the paper bag. The name printed on the wrapping was that of the most popular traditional sweet shop in the village. Their strawberry daifuku cakes were particularly popular. The shop only made four hundred a day, so they were impossible to get ahold of unless you were in line before the shop opened.

"Strawberry daifuku! We all lined up together!" Sarada sang happily as she arranged the sakura branches in a vase.

Boruto took the box from Mitsuki and ripped open the wrapping. Inside the wooden box, the strawberry daifuku sat neatly lined up, wrapped in washi paper.

You three lined up this morning for my sake? Konohamaru felt something warm rise up in his chest.

"I'll make some tea," Mitsuki said. "Where's the kitchen-ette area?"

"Oh, it's okay. I'll do it." Konohamaru held the boy back and grabbed the cane at the edge of the bed. "It's too depress-ing to be in here all the time. I'm glad to get out of this room."

As he stepped out of his hospital room, his students pulled out the round chairs stacked in one corner and sat down.

"I can't believe a ninja like Master Konoha would be hurt badly enough to have to stay in the hospital." Sarada sighed.

Mitsuki nodded. "It's fortunate that none of the passengers were injured, though."

Sarada turned on the TV. On the screen, a girl with golden hair was in the middle of an interview for the mid-morning news.

"Who's that?" Sarada frowned.

"Himeno Lily. You don't know her?" Boruto's eyes grew wide.

"I don't really watch TV. Who is she? Some kind of TV personality?"

"An idol. She's really popular right now. On TV all the

time." As he spoke, Boruto picked up a strawberry daifuku and peeled the paper away.

As if led by his example, Mitsuki and Sarada also reached out for a small cake.

That girl's an idol? Sarada gazed absently at the TV as she unwrapped her daifuku.

The girl on the screen was definitely cute. She wore white boots and a minidress with far more frills and ribbons than could ever be functional. Her golden hair had a gentle wave and reached down to her shoulders. Although she was probably at least fifteen, she spoke in a deliberately cute, innocent way that made her seem much younger.

An idol... I don't really care about that stuff. Still, I wonder what kinds of songs she sings? Thoughts drifting, Sarada took a bite of the daifuku and then jumped up as though she'd gotten an electric shock. "What is this?! It's so good!"

"It really is," Mitsuki agreed.

"Mm, it's great. But I like the zenzai my mom makes way better," Boruto said cheekily, even as he reached out for a second daifuku.

Aah, this strawberry daifuku. Amazing... Wow... Amazing... The delicious flavor sent Sarada into a reverie, and as she sunk her teeth into the small cake, she was lost in bliss. For a moment, she thought she should wait until Konohamaru came back to have another one, but two seconds later, she reconsidered and reached out again.

Music began to spill from the TV. Apparently, Lily was debuting her new song, "Marchmallow Heart."

Sarada looked at the song title displayed on the screen and felt a slight pain in her head.

Illuminated by colorful lights, Lily twisted her hips as she began to sing with a lisp.

Marchmallow Marchmallow Marshmalloooow ♪

Have a marshmallooow ♪ C'mon c'mon ♪
Go! Go! ♪ Go to ♪ Hell and angel ♪

"What even is this?!" Sarada cried out, unable to stand it any longer.

"Sarada, shut up." Boruto turned around, looking annoyed. "This is a hospital. You gotta be quiet."

"Th-these lyrics don't bother you at all? Like 'hell and angel' or 'Have a marshmallow, c'mon c'mon'? They don't even mean anything!"

"I don't care about the lyrics," he replied, finishing off his daifuku in a single bite. He was more interested in eating than the song.

"I mean, it's not like I especially care or anything," Sarada protested. "But, it's like, I can't help but get upset when they're actually putting these ridiculous lyrics on TV." She shot an angry glance at the screen. Lily was quite passionate in her performance as she crooned the nonsensical "Marchmallow puffy puffy puff puff puffaaaaa ♪."

"Aah! It's too much! I can't listen to this anymore!" Sarada brought her fist down on the remote control and the TV screen turned black.

"I guess. I thought it was a pretty interesting song, though." Mitsuki started to hum the melody.

I don't get boys. Still, this daifuku really is delicious. She nibbled at a strawberry daifuku while the three of them chatted until Konohamaru returned. He leaned on his cane, deftly carrying a tray of teacups in one hand.

"Ah?! You all just went ahead and ate without me?" Konohamaru laughed and handed each of his students a cup of tea.

"You find out anything about the guys who attacked the Thunder Train?" Boruto asked, sipping his tea. "Like the reason for the bombing? They committed multiple crimes, yeah?"

"Still nothing worthwhile," Konohamaru replied. "About the only clue we have is that they were wearing purple outfits. Also, they had excessively large holes in their ears."

"Holes?" Mitsuki asked, dubiously. "Do you mean like piercings?"

"Mm-hm. According to the medical team that examined the bodies, they each had five piercings in their ears, running from their ear lobes up into the cartilage."

"Is that to show they're part of a group? Like our headbands?"

"Can't say." Their team leader shrugged. "This is just the impression I got from fighting them, but I don't think they were all that threatening in terms of fighting power. Other than their boss, they were about at the chunin level. The tricky part about these guys was—"

"That they didn't hesitate to sacrifice themselves?" Sarada guessed.

"Exactly." Konohamaru nodded solemnly. "They chose death with their comrades over being caught and forced to give information. Trying to take guys like that alive is tough. Way more so than just killing them."

"It bugs me that they went out of their way to use actual bombs when they could have just used ninjutsu," Boruto remarked.

If this mysterious group's objective was an indiscriminate attack on villagers, there could be serious damage ahead if they didn't figure out some kind of countermeasures soon. If there was a bombing in the new city in the middle of the day when it was thronged with people...

There just wasn't enough information available to them. They couldn't know how urgent the situation was. At a loss for words, all four fell silent. The air in the hospital room was still.

"Maybe I'll have a strawberry daifuku!" Konohamaru said

brightly, trying to lift their spirits again. He lifted the lid, but the inside of the daifuku box was empty. "What?!"

Stunned, he checked the inside of the box four more times. But no matter how many times he looked, there was nothing in there.

"Y-you… What happened to the daifuku?" A tremor bleeding into his voice, he looked at his students.

"I only had two," Mitsuki asserted.

"I only had three," Sarada said.

"I only had four, okay?" Boruto noted casually.

"That adds up perfectly then, doesn't it?!" Konohamaru shot daggers at them with his eyes. "There were only nine of them! Come on!"

"Well, you know…" Sarada did feel guilty, but the daifuku really were delicious, so she didn't actually regret eating them. "W-we'll go get some more."

"No thanks. If you got the time for that, you should be training…" Although Konohamaru tried to put on a brave face, his shoulders were slumped.

"When will you be getting out of the hospital, Master?" Mitsuki said, changing the subject.

"The thing about that…" Konohamaru's face suddenly stiffened, and his eyes dropped to the cast on his right ankle. "The injury itself was no big deal, but I guess the bomb was rigged with a poison that induces a light paralysis. I have to stay here until the antidote does its work. Three weeks."

"Three weeks?" Sarada replied, concerned.

"What's gonna happen to our team in the meantime?" Boruto asked.

"Right. About that." Konohamaru glanced toward the door and smiled. "I've got a substitute taking over for me."

"A substitute?" Mitsuki asked.

"Don't worry." Konohamaru gave them a meaningful look.

"He's pretty strong. Well, that might be an understatement. He's *scary* strong."

"For real?!" Boruto clenched his hands in excitement. "I'm into it!"

"So who is this substitute?" Sarada asked, impatient with the little show Konohamaru was putting on.

A cool, low voice carried from one end of the room, clear as crystal. "Me."

The students knew who it was even before they turned to the door to see Sasuke, his face as expressionless as usual.

"No way!" Sarada cried. *Dad? Our master?!* She was over the moon, but quickly pulled herself back together. She cleared her throat. "Huh. So you're going to be our master, Dad?"

"Mm." He nodded. "It turns out I have to stay in the village for a while."

"Seriously? All right!" Boruto threw his arms up in the air with a grin that nearly split his face in two. His eyes glittered, and he didn't so much as try to hide his delight.

Next to him, Mitsuki smiled faintly, his face full of anticipation.

✖ ✖ ✖ ✖ ✖

Old Man Sasuke's gonna teach me ninjutsu!

Boruto couldn't control his excitement. His step had a lively bounce as he made his way to the part of the forest outside the village that had been designated as their training ground. He wanted to be a ninja like Sasuke some day, working to support the Hokage. The older ninja was his dream personified, and now he was going to be the team's master. There was no way Boruto was going to be able to keep his cool about the whole thing.

Boruto had received training from Sasuke before. It had

only been for a short time, but he'd learned a lot. That period of training was even the reason why he'd ended up rethinking his relationship with his father. Boruto treasured the time he'd spent with Sasuke.

I've gone on a bunch of missions since then, and I mean, I have to have grown a little. I'm definitely gonna show Old Man Sasuke how strong I've gotten!

This first day of training was going to be the stuff of his dreams.

✖ ✖ ✖ ✖ ✖

Whud krr krr krr krr! Zssshhrrrrrrrk!

Boruto stared speechless as Sasuke's kunai shot forward, systematically mowing down the trees of the forest before reducing the cliff rising up in the distance to rubble.

"A kunai can produce that much power?" Mitsuki murmured.

"Dad really is amazing," Sarada said. "Just how it is, you know?"

The cliff face slid off from the rest of the rock, kicking up a cloud of dust.

All that from one kunai?! How is that possible? Boruto was baffled.

Sasuke hadn't simply thrown the kunai. He'd kneaded his chakra with the kunai on one finger, and then, for an instant, released an electrical current. Boruto didn't really understand the mechanism, but in the blink of an eye, the kunai had flown off and shattered the distant cliff face.

Sasuke lowered his arm, looking cool and composed, and turned toward his students. "Maybe you're not yet ready to learn this technique, however."

A silent rebuttal rose up in all of their hearts—*So why'd you show it to us?*

Calmly, Sasuke pulled a handful of small dice from his leather bag. He distributed two each to Boruto and his comrades. "Your first task. Use ninjutsu to get doubles with these dice. You must not touch the dice."

All three looked at one other doubtfully.

"There are any number of ways," Sasuke said, tossing two dice into the air. He then pulled two shuriken out of his bag and flung them after the dice.

The shuriken flew through the air and grazed the corner of the two falling dice, knocking them down onto the grass. The spinning blades then arced around to boomerang back to Sasuke's hand.

The members of Team Seven crouched down and checked the faces of the dice: two sixes.

"Wow!" Boruto said, eyes round. Mitsuki also stared at the matched pair, while Sarada turned a smarmy smile on the two of them.

Not that it's any surprise, Boruto thought. *But Old Man Sasuke really is super amazing!*

✖ ✖ ✖ ✖ ✖

Thus, Boruto and the members of Team Seven applied themselves to the task of aligning the dice. With their dice set up on stumps and rocks, they each considered the best way to actually move the tiny cubes given their own particular talents and personalities.

"I'm going with shuriken," Sarada decided. She gently tossed a shuriken toward the dice on the stump.

Bam!

The blade slammed into the stump, missing the dice by a few centimeters. The air kicked up by the impact caused the dice to wobble, but not so much that either one rolled over. She decided she was aiming too wide and needed to tighten up a bit. This time, the shuriken hit the dice and split them each in two.

She took a closer look and found that the "dice" were actually sugar cubes marked with candy dots. They weighed almost nothing and would crumble at the slightest shock. She was going to have to move them with just the right amount of force—not too much, not too little—or she'd never be able to roll doubles.

Mitsuki had decided to use Wind Style and move the dice with a light breeze. He meant to nudge the sugar cubes with a gentle puff of air, but instead, the dice shot off into the forest.

"I'm strong with Rasengan!!" Boruto decided to make use of the flow of the Rasengan chakra to set his dice rolling. First, he created a small Rasengan in the palm of his hand. Even the slight pressure from this sent his dice flying, even though he hadn't so much as touched them yet. "Aaah…"

In order to get the dice to roll and the two faces to line up, he would have to hit both sugar cubes at the same time hard enough to move them, but not so hard that he crushed them or sent them shooting off into space. It seemed like an underwhelming and dull task, but it demanded incredibly fine control.

"Gah!"

"Hyah!"

"Ay!"

"Hah!"

"Aah, they broke again!"

"Dammit! I'm totally gonna do this!"

The three young ninja threw themselves into their training, complaining loudly all the while, as Sasuke stood back and watched them.

He couldn't help remembering his own training back when he was still a genin, those long days alongside Naruto and Sakura under Kakashi's tutelage. He'd only been attached to Team Seven briefly, and he'd wanted to become a ninja for different reasons from the rest of them. Even so, that brief period had laid deep roots inside of Sasuke, roots that held fast even now. With a wry smile, he realized he was, of all things, waxing nostalgic, which was very unlike him.

At the same time, however, he keenly felt how much the world—and with it the shinobi way of fighting—had changed since then. Gone was the turbulent era of war and blood spilled in vain, a time that had demanded brute strength of ninja and nothing else. Maintaining peace required not military might but rather diplomacy between a stable society and other countries. Necessary now was not simply a battle-ready ninja but one who could also react with clever statesmanship to whatever the situation demanded.

Through Naruto's efforts, the village of Konohagakure had changed. With the era of war at an end and trade thriving, the various countries had begun to share their progress and discoveries with each other, leading to remarkable modernization in the Land of Fire. Citizens could now go about their lives without worrying about their future or cowering in fear.

As the villagers of Konoha rejoiced in the peace, their memories of the world at war gradually faded. And they had long forgotten that one man had alone borne the burden of a crime and struck out at his own clan for the sake of peace in the village.

Sasuke had come to feel that it was best this way. He remembered his brother. That was enough. There was no need for the new generation to don mourning clothes as well. And as he watched Sarada, Mitsuki, and Boruto, he felt he could perhaps understand what had been going on his brother's mind when he'd sacrificed himself for the sake of the village.

This new generation of children had been nourished on the teachings of the village of Konohagakure. Sasuke felt a thrill of satisfaction at the idea that everything his brother had fought to keep safe was now being passed along to the younger citizens of the village. It made him believe that the long, long days and nights of war hadn't been in vain.

Education. Perhaps this was the most critical element in safeguarding their village and the country itself.

"Old Man Sasuke! You're the master. Give us a hint here!"

Sasuke abruptly lifted his face to meet a pair of carefree blue eyes, even bluer than the ones he was used to. "What's wrong, Boruto?"

"We tried Rasengan and shuriken and all kinds of stuff, but nothing's working. You gotta tell us how you did that with the shuriken!"

"A hint? Hmm…" Sasuke took a shuriken in one hand… and found himself at a loss for words. He performed the movement unconsciously, guided by his senses, the same as breathing. The whole thing was extremely difficult to describe. "You hold it like this…and throw it."

"That doesn't tell us anything at all!" Boruto stamped his feet in frustration.

"How do you adjust the force? A snap of the wrist? Or is it in your fingers?" Mitsuki asked.

"Mm." Sasuke stared at the palm of his own hand and thought for a minute. There probably was a hint he could give them, a trick to the whole process. But he only understood it intuitively. He struggled to teach it. "The way to adjust is…" He leaned forward. "Establish your target…and throw it like this." Even he knew that this told them absolutely nothing.

As the children sighed in perfect unison, Sasuke smiled wryly at himself. *I'm not suited to teaching.*

Kakashi had been great with words. While Sasuke simply

acted on instinct that defied explanation, Kakashi communicated all of his knowledge and experience to the next generation in an easy-to-understand manner.

I've got a long way to go as a master, Sasuke thought.

✖ ✖ ✖ ✖ ✖

In the end, Boruto wasn't able to get doubles with the dice, despite practicing until the sun went down. He had annihilated the powerful Momoshiki with his Rasengan, and yet he couldn't make a single sugar cube roll the way he wanted. It was humiliating.

Even after he got home, all he could think of was the dice training. Sitting in the bath, he remembered the day's practice and spread out his hands beneath the water. The droplets falling from the wet ceiling broke the surface above his palms. Just a tiny drop could cause a ripple in the water's surface. Maybe it wasn't impossible to hit the sugar cube with chakra without crushing it.

I can't get pysched out now! Boruto shook his head, reprimanding himself. *I only just started practicing. Too early to get bummed out! I'm Old Man Sasuke's student, after all!*

He held his wet hands in front of his eyes. "Gentle enough not to break the sugar cubes…" He'd only intended to do some visualization training, but he carelessly kneaded his chakra for real, and the water in the tub began to swirl into a vortex.

"Boruto?" His mother, Hinata, popped her head in immediately. "You can't go kneading chakra there. You'll break the tub."

"D-don't peep in the bath! Mom, you gotta stop using the Byakugan in the house!"

She giggled. "I didn't mean to. I just felt the presence of chakra."

By the time he got out of the bath, Himawari was watching a music show in the living room. On the screen, Himeno Lily was singing and dancing beneath colorful spotlights. Drops of sweat were flying off her.

"Have a marshmallooow ♪ C'mon c'mon ♪"

Himawari hummed along with Lily, her eyes glued to the screen.

"Himawari, you like Himeno Lily?" Boruto asked.

"Yeah!" Himawari nodded. "She's so cute. And she's a really good singer and dancer."

Is she? Boruto turned back to the screen, which was filled with a close-up on Lily's face. He didn't really get how she was cute, but he did think her eyes were a pretty color. Her deep-purple irises were bright and clear, almost like the color at the end of the rainbow.

Go! Go! ♪ Go tooo ♪ Hell and angel ♪
Go! Go! ♪ Go tooo ♪ Violet moon ♪

Hearing them again now, he had to admit Sarada was right—the lyrics were weird.

✘ ✘ ✘ ✘ ✘

The training with the dice continued the following day.

"Aaaaah!!" Sarada's pained cry echoed through the forest. The faces of the dice beside the shuriken plunged into the tree stump read three and four. "Almost doubles! I was so close…" She slumped to her knees.

"Heh heh! I'm totally gonna be the first to make it happen!" Boruto started boasting, lost in the moment. Then, "Ah!" His eyes widened in despair. He'd pushed too hard with the flow of chakra and split both of his dice in two.

"Maybe I'm closest to being the first one to do it," Mitsuki said with a laugh as he wove his signs to activate his Wind Style.

After watching his students desperately try anything and everything for a while, Sasuke called out to them, "Today, I'm adding something extra to the training schedule."

"Huh?" Boruto raised an eyebrow. "What?"

"Lorentz Gun."

What?

Both eyebrows now raised, he followed Sasuke as he led them to the top of a cliff. The front of the rock face he'd seen in the distance yesterday had been carved away by Sasuke's kunai and the ensuing a landslide.

"This technique is an application of Lightning Style."

Sasuke pulled out a brown kunai like the one he'd used before as his students bobbed their heads up and down.

"Hey, Dad?" Sarada asked. "Why's that kunai kinda red?"

"It's copper. It conducts electricity well." Sasuke readied the weapon in his hand. "With the traditional Lightning Style attack, you hit your opponent with a powerful voltage to cause damage. Boruto, your Purple Lightning is like that. But this technique is fundamentally different. It makes use of the fact that powerful electrical currents generate magnetic fields, a principle the scientific ninja team discovered recently. They're calling it *electromagnetic induction*."

Boruto scoffed at the words "scientific ninja team."

Sasuke turned toward the rock face in the distance and stretched out one of arm, balancing the kunai on his middle finger.

"Position the weapon in the direction of your target and set two bolts of electricity on either side." Electricity crackled upward from his palm. "Throw the copper kunai so that it passes between the two currents." He tossed the kunai.

Boom!

The instant the bolts on either side touched it, the kunai shot forward, fast enough that it shattered the sound barrier with a thunderous boom. It mowed down the trees of the forest and crashed into the rock face.

This technique generated a force that was on a different level from anything a bare hand could manage. Boruto doubted that the Hokage himself could throw a kunai faster.

Sasuke turned back to his stunned students. "First, try splitting the basic Lightning Style attack into two bolts of current. You want to generate a current in each hand at the same time."

"Okay!" Sarada and Mitsuki shouted in perfect unison.

Only Boruto stayed silent, looking glum as he glanced at the dust cloud that had enveloped the rock face.

Sasuke was not blind to Boruto's reaction, but he continued the lesson, pulling copper kunai out of his bag for each of his students. "Copper kunai are prone to rusting, so polish them regularly with vinegar. They're not as powerful when they're rusty."

"This is very interesting," Mitsuki said as he accepted the kunai. "A normal steel kunai is first heated in fire and then coated with a blackening film to protect it from rust. And yet a copper kunai is the opposite—you polish it in vinegar so that it doesn't rust."

"You know your stuff." Sasuke looked at Mitsuki, impressed.

"Master Konohamaru taught us about it."

"I knew that, too!" Sarada immediately staked her claim.

Rather than chiming in himself, Boruto stared at a bird in the sky.

"What's wrong?" Sasuke asked when Boruto didn't move to take the kunai from him.

"Oh, I'm gonna go practice moving the dice some more," he replied dully, and returned to the forest.

✖ ✖ ✖ ✖ ✖

Before he knew it, the western sky had taken on a faint red hue, and he hadn't managed to roll doubles even once.

I'm definitely gonna make it happen this time! Boruto held the dice in his hands as he kneaded his chakra.

The dice turned twice and then stopped, a three on each face.

I did it!

The thrill of victory was fleeting. A breath later, the die on the right slowly tumbled one more time to display a one.

"Gaaah! Come on!" Boruto kicked his legs out and flopped back. He'd been so close, which made it all the more vexing. "Aaah! Dammit!!"

I guess Sarada and Mitsuki are practicing that Lightning Style technique right about now. That electromagnetic whatever-it-is.

Boruto leaped to his feet, grabbed the dice, and flung them away, annoyed.

"Don't get so worked up."

The voice came from above his head. When he lifted his face, he saw Sasuke looking down on him.

"I wasn't… It's not like that." Knowing how dejected he sounded, Boruto quickly averted his eyes upward. A crow glided through the air above them.

Sasuke sat down on a stump. Instead of looking at Boruto, he also directed his gaze up toward the sky. "Boruto. You hate science?"

"Why would you think that?"

"Just a hunch."

Dyed orange, the sky seemed almost on fire, and the wind coming at them was brisk. Even so, it was a peaceful sunset. The grass swayed in the breeze, and their long shadows rippled in slight waves.

"It's not that I hate it. It's just…" Boruto began to speak

slowly, feeling guilty somehow. "It's just like…all that stuff about making it last with blackening, and the Lorentz Gun and all that… Relying on science, it's so un-ninja-like. I mean, it's not very…cool."

"You don't think so?"

"Yeah… I don't actually like science."

Rolling clouds blocked the setting sun, casting shadows on Boruto and Sasuke until the gentle breeze slowly pushed them away.

"If you know science, you can use ninjutsu even more effectively." Sasuke watched a bird returning to its nest as he spoke. "Science and ninjutsu aren't in opposition. They grow from the same roots."

Boruto lowered his eyes and glared at the ground. "I know." He was thinking about a bitter memory from his chunin exams when he'd secretly used a forbidden scientific ninja tool and was disqualified after being discovered by none other than his own father. In his head, he knew science was definitely not a bad thing, just like Sasuke said. But his irrational heart rejected the whole idea out of hand. Just hearing "science" brought back his guilt over the exams.

"Boruto, you're an excellent ninja," Sasuke said. "You've been blessed with an excellent education, and you've got the talent and determination to go with it. If the ninja who have died protecting the village could see you, I'm sure they would be proud."

"As if!!" Boruto spat. He was certain Sasuke was just being nice, which only made him feel more pathetic. "All those generations of ninja! They'd laugh at me, living this easy life, science everywhere."

"Of course they wouldn't. This kind of peace, this progress, was exactly what the warring era ninja dreamed of while they spent those long hours studying and honing their skills."

He pulled a kunai from his pocket. Protected from rusting, it emitted a dull light. "By burnishing the kunai, you keep it from corroding. A special power causes it to accelerate when you throw it between two bolts of electricity. Just to obtain this meager knowledge, so many of our predecessors made countless observations, did endless analyses. The scientific ninja tools are the grand sum of this accumulation of knowledge. True, it wasn't appropriate for you to use one in the chunin exams, but they can be a powerful weapon in actual battle. A force to protect the village."

The clouds slid along above them. and Sasuke and Boruto were once more bathed in the light of the setting sun. Sasuke's normally black hair and eyes shone a strange orange.

"Many people spent many years building up this knowledge base. And Boruto, it's your generation on the frontlines now." Sasuke suddenly looked at him, and their eyes met. When Boruto averted his gaze, Sasuke's face softened. "I know you hate science. I must be boring you."

"Well, you know... You're sure talking an awful lot, Old Man Sasuke."

"Not as much as your father."

Boruto looked off at where he'd thrown the dice into the bushes earlier. A line of ants now stretched out from the shattered sugar cubes.

He wanted to live up to Sasuke's expectations, so much so that it hurt. Which was exactly why he was frustrated that he just couldn't get past this visceral hatred of science.

"It will be dark soon. We'll head back to the village." Sasuke stood up and started walking toward the cliff where Sarada and Mitsuki were training. Boruto followed him without a word.

�҉ ✣ ✣ ✣ ✣

That night, Mitsuki stood alone on the branch of a massive tree, training on his own with the Lorentz Gun. He was able to generate the Lightning Style bolts, but they scattered the instant they came into contact with the air. Left to its own devices, an electric current would melt away into nothing. Holding one in the form of a bolt took real skill.

The sky was quite clear. The half-moon shining sharply above the treetop looked like it was floating right in front of his nose.

Crackle crackle…

Mitsuki concentrated on the image of a pillar, centering his electric current as he practiced generating the Lightning Style.

"That's a pretty interesting bit of training, hm?"

The sudden voice from behind interrupted his focus. He looked back to find Orochimaru standing on a branch above his, looking down at him.

"What? Don't you have anything better to do?"

"I was taking a walk," Orochimaru chuckled. "The moon was so beautiful."

"Mm-hm." Mitsuki raised an eyebrow. "And you came all the way here."

"From what I saw, it looks like you're trying to control the flow of Lightning Style. But to what end?"

Eager to get back to his training, Mitsuki was being noncommittal in his responses, but Orochimaru kept talking. Apparently, he really didn't have anything better to do.

"By controlling the flow of Lightning Style, you can use a magnetic field to accelerate objects."

"Mm, I see." Orochimaru nodded. "Electromagnetic induction?"

Mitsuki ignored him and focused his mind on the palm of his hand. He envisioned a straight line as he tried to pull in the current that was so intent on scattering. The electricity in his hand crackled and stretched out as far as he could see, wrapped in plasma.

I did it!

The instant the thought crossed his mind, the current popped with a loud crack.

"Gah!" Too excited by his apparent success, he'd accidentally relaxed his mind.

"Not too shabby." Orochimaru nodded with satisfaction. "Well, you are my son, after all. It's only natural you'd be able to do this much at least."

"I still have a long way to go. I can't maintain the form. I'll need time to shape the electricity how I want it. It won't be in an instant like Sasuke."

"What?" The color of Orochimaru's eyes abruptly changed. "Mitsuki…is Sasuke training you?"

"Didn't I mention that? Master Konohamaru's in the hospital, so Sasuke's filling in."

"Hmm. *The* Sasuke," Orochimaru muttered. "Perhaps I will come watch your training tomorrow."

"Don't you dare."

✖ ✖ ✖ ✖ ✖

With the dice and the Lorentz Gun and everything else, Sasuke's training covered a lot of ground. He subjected them to all kinds of things, from drilling the basics to mock battles.

By the fifth day of training, the three students were more or less able to get doubles with their dice—perhaps not nine times out of ten, but at least once or twice. Sarada and Mitsuki were also drawing steadily closer to mastering the Lorentz Gun.

But Boruto still continued to avoid science, despite knowing that having science and the natural order on his side was going to be even more important as a ninja in this new era.

As long as he shied away from it, he'd inevitably fall behind the other ninja. And he did want to overcome his aversion to science, but he couldn't do anything about how he felt. He knew Sasuke was worried about how stubbornly he turned his back to science, as he himself was.

One morning, at the beginning of their second week of training, Sasuke arrived thirty minutes after their usual start time.

"You're a lot more comfortable with the finer control, hm?" he called when he saw his students already facing their sugar-cube dice, practicing on their own. "Keep practicing this every day until you succeed every single time. Mitsuki, Sarada, don't forget your Lorentz Gun training. Also, basic drills and mock battles every day. If you want to incorporate anything else into your training, talk it over and decide from there."

"What's up, Old Man Sasuke?" Boruto turned toward their teacher. "Sounds like you're going somewhere."

"Mission came in," Sasuke replied. "I'm setting out now."

"What?!" Sarada cried out, her eyes wide. "You're leaving the village?"

"Mm. To do an emergency survey. I'll be back in about a week."

"That's pretty sudden." Boruto frowned.

"Hey, Dad?" Sarada glared up at Sasuke without blinking. "Did you tell Mom? Does she know you're going away?"

"Mm."

"Really?" She sounded doubtful. "When did you tell her?"

"I talk plenty with Sakura after you've gone to bed." Sasuke smiled wryly. "So don't worry."

"Really…"

The details of Sasuke's mission were, as always, top secret, and although Boruto pestered him, their teacher would tell them absolutely nothing.

When Sasuke left on his mission through the village gates,

they watched until they could no longer see him, then went to get lunch at Ichiraku Ramen. After filling their stomachs, they pushed past the curtains in the doorway and returned to their training area.

Compared to the relaxed atmosphere of the old town, the new town and all its impressive new developments were busy day and night. Streetlamps shone down on the newly laid roads where boutiques with big show windows stood alongside cafes with open patios. A clerk called out the day's specials in front of the traditional sweet shop, and in the center of the crossroads, a cat mascot was handing out some kind of pamphlet.

"So like, that anmitsu I ate at with Cho-Cho was super good."

"Cho-Cho's a big old rice ball herself, though. It's cannibalism. She's a cannibal."

"I don't know if I'd put it like that."

They were walking along, lost in conversation, when a pamphlet was thrust before them. Boruto reflexively reached to take it, and a giant ball of flesh grabbed hold of his hand.

"Ah?!" Lifting his face in surprise, he stared up at the cat mascot.

The cat brought its face in close to Boruto's ear. In a low voice, it said, "You three are ninja, right?"

"Yeah, b-but…" Boruto stammered. "What's with you?"

"I have a favor to ask!" The cat mascot dragged Boruto by his hand into a back alley. Sarada and Mitsuki hurried after them.

The narrow alley was damp and deserted—of people, anyway. A real cat curled up on top of an oil drum fled, looking annoyed.

The cat mascot turned meekly back to the three ninja. "The truth is, I'm a little bit famous."

But you're a cat.

"Someone's trying to kill me!"

But you're a cat.

"I want you to protect me! I can pay!"

But you're a cat.

The three ninja looked at one another doubtfully.

"Um, maybe we should go to the hospital first." Mitsuki said as smoothly as possible.

The cat stomped on the ground. "I really am in trouble." She popped off her costume's head. Bright, wavy, golden hair came tumbling out.

The ninja gaped, three jaws dropping at once.

"Please...don't let me die in a place like this!" pleaded Himeno Lily.

CHAPTER 2

SASUKE'S STORY: STAR PUPIL

2

"Let's not just stand out here on the street talking," Himeno Lily said, before leading took Boruto and his teammates to a brand-new high-rise condominium in the new town. As they slipped through the brightly lit, glass-walled entryway, the concierge stationed there simply bowed, entirely unfazed by Lily's attire.

Lily held up an ID card when they got in the elevator, not bothering to push any buttons. Boruto scratched his head at this, only to discover that the elevator went straight to her apartment. When the doors opened with a ding, he found himself looking into her living room.

"Huh? Uh? What about our shoes?" The lack of an entry-way baffled him.

"You can just leave them on," Lily replied.

It was almost vulgar how large the tiled living room was. The space was filled with a TV as big as a futon and a grand piano that was pink for some reason. Stuffed rabbits and bears sat snugly together on an expensive-looking leather sofa.

As Boruto whirled his head back and forth to take it all in,

Lily put some tea on and then moved a number of the stuffed animals to the top of the piano to make space for them all to sit on the sofa.

Boruto took a sip of tea and grimaced. "It's sweet!"

"It's chocolate tea. Cute, isn't it?"

It seemed that those strange creatures known as *idols* were driven to seek out cuteness even in their tea.

Boruto stared incredulously once more at Lily sitting before him. Wavy golden hair, sharp purple eyes. Himeno Lily herself, from the other side of the TV screen.

"So maybe you could explain things to us then?" Mitsuki asked, looking straight at Lily. He didn't touch his tea. "Could you tell us why on earth you would go so far as to dress up in a cat costume to talk to us?"

"Right." Her voice somber, Lily set out a piece of paper the size of a business card. "This arrived for me this morning."

The short message was written in slanted characters, as if with the help of a ruler: *If you don't cancel Bewitching Macaron Night, we will kill Himeno Lily during the show. This is your first and final warning.*

"Bewitching Macaron Night?" Sarada raised a doubtful eyebrow.

"It's the name of my upcoming show," Lily replied.

"There's the possibility that it's a prank," Mitsuki suggested, examining the card. "Did you talk to your agency about this?"

"I haven't said anything yet!" she cried. "I don't want to tell them. My agency's hardheaded. They'll cancel the show."

"I think that'd be the right choice, though." Sarada's gaze was cold.

"I have to do the show!" Lily scrunched her face up in a pout. "All the fans who are on this journey with me… If I up and cancel right before the show, I just know they'll leave me!"

"They're not going to leave you over something like that," Boruto muttered.

"Idol fans are creatures of extremes!" Lily leaned toward him forcefully. "They only have two settings: they love you or they hate you. They watch my every movement. If I mess up in any way, any way at all, they'll happily cut me loose."

"Still, it'd be better to put in a proper request through the formal channels," Sarada said gently.

Lily shook her head. "The Hokage's wise! Do you really think he'd let the show go on just because a selfish idol like me wants it to? I just know he'd cancel the whole thing!" she said, displaying some self-awareness.

"So you came to talk to us instead," Sarada said.

"Yes. I thought I could get a ninja to protect me behind the scenes if I went and asked one directly. And...and you're Team Seven! You're special! Boruto, the oldest son of the Seventh Lord Hokage, with Hyuga blood in his veins! Sarada, Uchiha descendant, daughter to Haruno Sakura, a student of the Fifth Hokage! You—you're kind of a mystery, Mitsuki. I don't know much about you, but I get the feeling that you're something super special! Also, you all seem really nice!"

"You've really checked us out." Sarada looked doubtful again.

"That last reason is probably the whole of it, hm?" Mitsuki muttered, exasperated.

Boruto felt exasperated too. Although he was normally happy to listen to praise being heaped on him and his family, he could feel nothing but suspicion in this situation.

Lily's purple eyes filled with tears. "If it's about money, I can pay. I haven't used any of the salary I've been getting since I became an idol. I've saved all of it." She thrust a check out at them.

"It's not about money—" Boruto started, and then spotted

the row of zeros squeezed onto the check. *One, ten, hundred, thousand...* He whistled under his breath. How many Extreme Ninja cards could he get with all this?

"We can't take money for an unofficial mission!" Sarada's voice brought him back to reality.

"Yeah. We can't take that," Mitsuki agreed.

"What?!" Lily opened her eyes opened wide and put a hand to her mouth. "Does that mean you'll take my case for no pay at all?!"

"How is it you only hear what you want?!" Sarada shouted. "It means *we...won't...do it!*"

"Please..." Lily's bottom lip quivered. "I'll do anything. Oh! How about I get you some VIP tickets for my concert?!"

"Why would we want that?!" Sarada's eyes narrowed dangerously.

Setting aside the matter of pay, Boruto's mind immediately leaped to Himawari and how her eyes had shined as she sstared at Lily on that singing show. He was sure she'd be crushed if something happened at the concert, or if Lily had to stop performing for good. And not just Himawari. All of Lily's fans in the village of Konoha.

"H-hey!" Boruto said awkwardly. "Let's take this one! We can't just leave a person in trouble like this!"

"What? Where is this coming from, Boruto?" Sarada regarded him suspiciously.

"N-nowhere. It's just, as ninja, we can't exactly let this go."

"I wasn't saying we should do nothing," she sighed. "But if we're going to take a mission, it should be after we talk to the Lord Hokage."

"The Hokage's in a tough place, though. He's responsible for the village. He can't really take risks, y'know? This is exactly when we genin gotta step up and be more flexible about stuff!"

The image of Sasuke flitted through the back of his mind. Boruto was behind Sarada and Mitsuki in their training, but if they succeeded in guarding Lily while Sasuke was away, Boruto was sure his teacher would see how skilled he really was.

"Well, you do have a point." Sarada's attitude softened in the face of his powerful enthusiasm. "What do you think, Mitsuki?"

"If Boruto says he wants to do it, then I'm happy to go along with that."

It was settled. Boruto was grateful to his teammates and the value they placed on their friendship.

Sarada finished her chocolate tea. "Okay. We gotta make a plan then."

"Where's the venue?" Mitsuki asked.

"Konoha Dome!" Lily gleefully pulled out a pamphlet. "They just finished it last month! It's that dome-shaped stadium. The polycarbonate roof opens and closes, so it can be totally open air, and the concourse is decked out like a hotel. It's a total dream venue! It's got a fifty-thousand person capacity!"

Bam!

Sarada slapped a hand on the low table, making the cups jump. "That's way too dangerous! Fifty thousand people means every assassin in the world could walk right in and hide in plain sight. You're practically asking them to kill you!"

"That's why I want to hire you," Lily protested. "Oh! Right! Is that thing about the Uchiha clan using the Sharingan to look for suspicious peo—"

"My eyes are not some kind of surveillance camera!" Sarada looked like she might be about to pop a blood vessel.

"So, like, Lily?" Mitsuki said after a few minutes of quiet thought. "Your top priority is to sing, right?"

"Yes!"

"Not be in the spotlight or have everyone looking at you, right?"

"Yes!"

"Are you going to be singing live?"

"No! I'll be lip-syncing, of course!"

"I see," Mitsuki murmured, and turned his gaze toward Boruto. "Then we'll just have to have Boruto do the heavy lifting."

"What?" Boruto raised his eyebrows.

Mitsuki patted his shoulder. "You're going to take the stage dressed as Lily."

✖ ✖ ✖ ✖ ✖

"You're doing it wrong, Boruto. You have to be more catlike in that final pose. Show the audience your toe beans. Be all 'meooow.' And you have to really put your hips into it when you're blowing kisses. Otherwise the love won't reach the people in the back."

"I seriously have no idea what you're even talking about…" Boruto's shoulders slumped, and a ribbon attached to the Alice band on his head slid down to the ground. Tortured by the spectacle of wearing high heels, he still managed to squat down and pick it up. He was wearing the outfit Lily had planned to wear to Bewitching Macaron Night: a puffy dress that reached down to the middle of his calves, a checkered jacket, and silver stiletto heels with sequins sewn on top, as if they weren't already sparkly enough already.

"You can do this, Boruto. The success of our plan is all up to you." Mitsuki offered up this bit of encouragement as if he were entirely removed from the situation. Boruto glared at him.

Believing it far too risky to let Lily take the stage, Mitsuki had proposed that they use a double instead. Boruto was the lucky stand-in. Disguised as Lily, he would stand in the spotlight and move his mouth while the idol spoke from the wings between songs. Meanwhile, Sarada would search the crowd with her Sharingan, and Mitsuki would grab anyone who looked suspicious.

"Boruto, you're so cute!" Sarada squealed. "You look like a girl."

"Shut up!" he snarled. "Why aren't you the one doing this?"

"If you can use the Sharingan, I'll gladly trades places."

Boruto couldn't argue with that. Naturally, he had firmly rejected Mitsuki's plan when he'd first heard it—"No way I'm dressing up as a girl!"—but when pressed, he'd been unable to come up with any alternatives.

So he'd ended up taking on the role of Lily's double.

Marchmallow Marchmallow Marshmalloooow ♪
Have a marshmallow ♪ *C'mon c'mon* ♪

Now Boruto found himself having to learn the choreography for "Marchmallow Heart" and the other twelve songs in the set list for the big day.

"Boruto." Lily sighed. "Please move your eyes around more evenly. Lily belongs to everyone."

"There's gonna be fifty thousand people. I can't look at every single one of them…"

"You have to look at them. With determination. That one moment is eternal for the audience."

"What are you even talking about?" Boruto didn't understand ninety percent of what Lily said, but he dilligently put his athletic abilities to work in order to master her lessons. Learning the dances wasn't especially hard, nor was the between-song banter any real challenge. The issues were his pride and his shame.

Whenever Boruto started to feel pathetic or to lose heart, he reminded himself that this was all for the sake of peace in the village—and to get Sasuke to notice him. *I can hardly call myself a ninja if I get hung up on my pride and lose sight of my objective.*

By the day before the live show, he'd somehow managed to hammer the basics of being Himeno Lily into his head.

"You really did learn the whole thing in a week. Although I'd expect nothing less of a Konoha ninja." Lily was thoroughly impressed with Boruto's efforts.

"Well, it's for the sake of the mission. When Old Man Sasuke gets back, I wanna stand tall and make our report to him!"

"Old Man Sasuke?" Lily asked. "Do you mean Sarada's father, Uchiha Sasuke?"

"Yup! Old Man Sasuke's my master!" Boruto declared happily.

Smiling, Lily narrowed her eyes. "So Sasuke's your teacher then."

"Do you have one?" he asked in return. "Like, an idol teacher?"

"I do." She nodded. "Someone who inspired me to try to be an idol. I haven't seen him in a long time… But he's still my teacher, even now."

Was she talking about a producer or something? He was curious, but the something about that faraway look in her eyes kept Boruto from asking her anything more.

✕ ✕ ✕ ✕ ✕

The day of Bewitching Macaron Night arrived. A long line stretched out from the entrance to the dome, waiting to go inside. The audience was uniformly dressed in Lily's preferred shocking pink, large fans and pen lights in hand, eager for the doors to open.

A shadowy figure looked down on the excited group. Cloak flapping in the wind, he sent his gaze racing over the surroundings, searching for something. The fans below were utterly absorbed in their excitement, and not one of them noticed Uchiha Sasuke.

✕ ✕ ✕ ✕ ✕

"Whoa! There's a ton of people." Astonished, Boruto watched on the monitor in the dressing room as the audience seats filled up.

"Well, of course. It's actually sold out!" Lily held her head high.

With pink lightsticks in hand, the capacity crowd looked like they could hardly wait for the show to start.

Boruto noticed a large camera set up in the middle of the first floor seats. It bore the logo of a TV program he'd actually appeared on himself. "That's a TV camera."

"Looks like. I guess the show is going to be broadcast on a music program," Lily explained nervously.

"What?!" Boruto's eyes flew open. "You didn't tell us that!"

"I'm sorry. I only just found out myself…"

"Gotta make sure my jutsu holds." He felt a touch of anxiety run through him, but the audience was already inside the dome. He couldn't turn back now.

The start time was fast approaching. Boruto moved to the wings of the stage with Lily. The staff had already been informed of what was going on and had promised to keep quiet about the switch.

Boruto transformed into Lily, grabbed the hem of his skirt between two fingers, and walked gracefully out into the center of the semi-circular stage. Chilly smoke rolled down around him and off the edge. In the stiletto heels, Boruto stood nearly ten centimeters taller than usual.

"Boruto, your face is too stiff." In his earpiece, he could

hear the voice of Lily watching from the wings. "Everyone in the audience is your lover. Please look at them with love."

"But the seats are pitch black. I can't see faces," he whispered.

"If you look with your heart's eyes, you'll see them."

As usual, he had no idea what she meant, but he'd come this far—he just had to get out there and finish it now. He got into position, marked in phosphorescent tape on the floor. The smoke chilled his feet, but his head, caught in the beam of the spotlight, was hot. He could sense the excitement of the thousands of people on the other side of the thick curtain as though they were generating electricity. When he really thought about it, it was actually kind of amazing that this many people would come all this way just to hear someone sing some songs. Every person there was the fan of a single girl. They had come to see Himeno Lily. Not Boruto.

"Hey, Lily?" Boruto said into the headset. "Are you sure you're okay not being out here?"

"What?"

"It's just, you became an idol because you wanted to see this, yeah? I can't believe you're actually satisfied just watching from the wings."

"This is enough for me." Her response was immediate.

He wondered if that was really the case. "So why did you want to become an idol anyway?"

The curtain went up. A galaxy of shocking pink stars flashed before him. The cheer that rose up was deafening.

"Lily? Can you hear me?" He was starting to wonder if there was something wrong with the earpiece when he heard Lily's voice, hesitant.

"I wanted to follow my master's teachings."

"Hey, I've been wanting to ask you—"

A round pin light snapped onto him, and an incredibly loud

upbeat tune began to play. The guitar intro of the first song. He cut the conversation short. Face vibrating at the rattling noise, Boruto gripped the microphone—powered off, naturally—and took the first step of the dance he'd worked so hard to memorize.

✖ ✖ ✖ ✖ ✖

In the arena seats Lily had gotten them, Sarada and Mitsuki waited for the show to start. The standing seats were split into six blocks of two rows and three columns. Blocks A, B, and C were in front, while blocks D, E, and F were to the rear. Their seats were around the center of the B block, toward the front of the center of the arena. To blend in, they both had lightsticks in one hand and fans that read "Lily, over here! ♥" and "I love you, Lily!" in the other.

Mitsuki was covering one eye with his hand as per the plan. They were on the look out for anyone suspicious, but at the moment, everyone looked like typical idol fans.

"Hey, Mikki! Isn't that a TV camera over there?" Sarada pointed at the camera crew in the center of the first floor seats. "Lily didn't say anything about a live broadcast..."

"We'll just have to keep a low profile as we look for the assassin so that no one notices us," he replied.

The lights started to go down in anticipation of the start of the concert.

Sarada willed herself to relax and opened her eyes wide. They shone with a reddish light, and her pupils shrunk like a cat on the hunt. Shadows in the shape of magatama popped up in her irises like inverted commas. The Sharingan, the unusual power she'd inherited from her father, allowed her to see through anything and everything in this world, and now she used it to scan the crowd.

Behind them, she spotted two people carrying a metal pipe-like instrument, likely some kind of firearm. She couldn't sense any chakra.

"I see them. Guys with a gun. Probably not ninja. Location...block F, last row."

"Let's go!" Mitsuki darted away through the audience. The area was pitch black now that all the lights were down, but because he'd kept one eye covered while the lights were still up, his eyes were already accustomed to the darkness.

According to Lily, they had about thirty-five seconds between the house lights going down and the stage lights popping on. They would need no more than ten to make it to the F block. However, they weren't even out of the B block when the stage suddenly grew bright.

"What?!" Mitsuki cried.

"This isn't what she told us!" Sarada snarled. "That Lily—!"

It hadn't even been ten seconds, and already the introductory banter was blaring at them as smoke spilled over the edge of the stage and into the audience.

"We got trouble! They're on the move!" Sarada shouted, watching the gun-toting men with her Sharingan. "They're taking the long way around. Probably headed for the right side of block A! They're going to shoot from the front row!"

"But we can't move!" Mitsuki groaned.

The crowd had turned into a crush of people, pressing in closer from all directions and trapping the two ninja in place. But they couldn't exactly go tossing civilians aside, and if they tried to use any ninjutsu, it would be captured on camera.

"Lily! Over here!"

"Lily! You're the best!"

The wild enthusiasm of the audience quickly took over and anything resembling order vanished.

We have to do something. We have to get to the front row right now! Jammed in amongst the surging bodies, Sarada frantically scanned their surroundings and saw something strange—a person surfing along on top of the crowd. Their prone body was held up and passed from fan to fan so that it moved slowly toward the stage at the front of the venue. The members of the audience seemed perfectly at ease with this body gliding along above their heads. In fact, they worked together like a well-oiled machine, as though this were the most natural thing in the world. Was this just something that happened at idol shows?

"We'll get them to carry us, too!" Mitsuki shouted.

"Huh?" Sarada couldn't believe what she was hearing.

"It's the only way we can get anywhere near those guys without revealing that we're ninja!" He had no sooner spoken than he was kicking at the ground and jumping up onto the shoulders of the person in front of him. "Gotta surf!"

The cool and collected Mitsuki she was familiar with disappeared. Now she watched as he spread his arms and dove on top of the audience, shouting like an excited fan.

"Whoa! Hold him up! Let him ride!"

The wild fans held Mitsuki's body up and passed him forward.

What?! I had no idea Mitsuki was that kind of guy… But whoa. I can't do that. No way.

Vehemently opposed to any kind of human surfing, Sarada cast about for another route to the front of the crowd, but stopped when she caught sight of Boruto on stage. Bathed in the spotlight, he was dancing in a dress and heels, sweat shining on his forehead.

Did her own personality even matter in the face of a mission? Neither Boruto nor Mitsuki was even slightly accustomed to any of this, but they were both fighting hard, no matter how dorky they looked.

This is no time for me to get all uptight. She leaped up onto a fan's shoulders. She could feel the passionate intensity of the excited crowd below. *This is scary! I really don't want to do this! But I've got no choice!*

"L-Lily, you're the super best!" Sarada shouted awkwardly. She spread her arms out and dove into the audience. Instantly, a swarm of hands sprang up around her body and began to whisk her away to the stage.

She felt like a bamboo leaf flowing down a river. It was a strange, itchy sensation, but it was the fastest way to the stage. She was going to get there ahead of those men.

She lifted her head slightly and looked toward block A, then frowned when she realized she couldn't see the men anymore. She quickly scanned the area, but there was no sign of them. Had they changed their route?

"Mitsuki!" she called out in a tense voice as Lily's fans carried her along. "The target's on the move!"

"Where?!" he shouted back.

She narrowed her eyes to seek them out, but everyone was waving fans and jumping up and down, which made it hard to see.

"Aah! You're all in the way!" Sarada cried in annoyance and opened her eyes wide.

Sharingan!

Instantly, her field of view opened up. The movement of the people around her became crystal clear. Apparently, the gunmen had given up on the front row because of the crowd and were now racing up the stairs to the second floor.

"They're headed upstairs!"

"Let's hurry!"

The ninja sat up on the wave of people and shifted until

they were both moving the way they wanted to go. They were still able to make it look as though the crowd was carrying them as they crawled along on top of upthrust palms toward their targets.

At the central aisle that separated blocks A, B, and C from blocks D, E, and F, they dropped to the ground. The passage was partitioned off by a fence. The air was less stuffy here, and Sarada breathed a sigh of relief.

The second-floor seats protruded out over the rear block, so the only way to get to the stairs up from this central corridor was to head out into the concourse, through the doors to the rear, and then go around.

"Looks like we're going to have to dive again," Sarada said wearily.

"No." Mitsuki shook his head. "There's no need for that."

She gasped with sudden realization when she saw Mitsuki pressing on one eye. The current song—"Woo Woo ★ Love Fantasy Train"—was almost over. Once it ended, the lights would go out temporarily, and the cameras wouldn't be able to see them in the dark.

Woo woo! Woo woo! Lovely star beam ♪
Woo woo! Woo woo! Milky moon sexy ♪

With one hand still over his eye, Mitsuki grabbed Sarada with his other. The gunmen were still crouching to the rear of the second-floor seats, perhaps getting into position to fire. The song ended, the lights went out, and the area was plunged into darkness.

Mitsuki stretched his arm toward the second-floor seats and grabbed hold of the railing. Still holding Sarada, he contracted his arm and the two of them swung upward like Tarzan and Jane.

The second floor was much calmer than the arena floor. Most of the people were sitting in their seats. Mitsuki and

Sarada crawled along the narrow aisle until they reached the rear. The men were there, waiting for the lights to come back on. One of them held the gun. Neither appeared to be able to see in the dark. Sarada went around to the front while Mitsuki took the rear.

"Okay, next song! Here we go!" Lily's voice came from the wings of the stage, and the lights flooded back on.

At the same time, Sarada yanked away the gun. Before either man could so much as gasp in surprise, Mitsuki chopped at the napes of their necks. Both fell forward, unconscious.

Mitsuki grabbed them by their collars and laid them out in the aisle. Their eyes had rolled all the way back in their heads. They were down for the count.

"Mission complete, huh?" Sarada said as she took the bullets out of the gun.

Hyoo! Something grazed her hair.

"Huh?" When she looked back in surprise, she heard the whoosh of air once more, and the bodies of the men in the aisle bounced slightly. She watched as a pool of red liquid slowly spread out beneath them. Both men now bore holes in their foreheads.

Mitsuki quickly pressed his cuffs up against the wounds to try and stop the bleeding, but the gunmen were already dead.

"Someone took them out," she breathed. "To shut them up?"

"But from where exactly?!"

It was too perfectly organized. Sarada activated her Sharingan again and sent her gaze racing around the area. The audience was utterly focused on the stage, so no one had noticed that anything strange was going on.

They were as far back as you could get in venue. There were only a limited number of positions for a sniper to be targeting them from: the spotlight above the stage, the lighting booth on the second floor, or...

"There!" She pointed at the roof of Konoha Dome.

"They're shooting from there?" Mitsuki narrowed his eyes in that direction, but because the polycarbonate was fairly opaque, there was no way he'd be able to spot their shooter with the naked eye.

But Sarada could see the figure of a man bearing a rifle with a scope just fine. He was lying flat on the roof, loading the rifle. There was a hole about the size of a tennis ball in the double polycarbonate roof, which the man was using to shoot into the arena.

Reflexively, Sarada reached for a shuriken, but stopped herself. "He's too far away. What are we supposed to do now?"

✘ ✘ ✘ ✘ ✘

I hope Sarada and Mitsuki are getting it done!

Even as he fretted, Boruto perfectly inhabited the role of Lily, although the tips of his toes were already throbbing in pain from being wedged into the stiletto heels. From the stage, he couldn't see what was going on in the audience, which only added to his anxiety.

"We'll do the call and response once this song ends, so please take action pattern B, Boruto."

Lily's instructions coming through the earpiece were ceaseless. He desperately tried to remember all the gestures he'd practiced with her. He was pretty sure action pattern B was lifting an arm up, snapping his fingers together, and making a cute face. He awkwardly raised his hand.

"Are you all ek-chited?!" Lily shouted from the wings into the microphone in time with his movement.

Chited? The unfamiliar word baffled him momentarily, but it was clearly what the audience wanted to hear. They threw their hands up enthusiastically.

"Yaaah!"

"Okay then! Wet's go to da necht shong!"

Shong?! Boruto was perplexed once more as the speakers directly behind him started in with the upbeat opening.

✄ ✄ ✄ ✄ ✄

"There's a way," Mitsuki murmured, glaring up at the sniper on the dome. "But the audience will see, even during a blackout. The cameras, too."

"We're probably thinking the same thing."

The Lorentz Gun. If she used the technique they'd only just learned from Sasuke, she could reach the top of the dome with room to spare.

But there were two risks. The first was that chances of success were low. The technique was composed of two separate actions: generating contained bolts of electricity and throwing a kunai. Sasuke was able to pull it all off by himself, but Sarada and her teammates had a long way to go before they could manage the same feat. They'd made it work a few times during training by splitting the technique into its component parts, with Mitsuki providing the electric charge and Sarada throwing the kunai. But they still hadn't gotten to the point where they could precisely target a given location and actually hit it.

The other risk was the fact that they would undoubtedly be exposed as genin. They'd definitely be censured for having let the two assassins die, but if they were exposed to the crowd, that would be the end of the live show Lily so desperately wanted.

"We can't just sit here and do nothing," Mitsuki said crisply in the face of Sarada's hesitation.

"You're right. I guess we've just gotta do it." Sarada gripped a kunai, and Mitsuki stretched out his hands, ready to generate the required current.

"Sarada, if the Lorentz Gun succeeds, leave the venue right away. We'll tell them it was just me and Boruto who accepted this mission."

"What? No way. Absolutely not." She shook her head.

Mitsuki sighed. "I figured you'd say that." He steadied his hands and plasma crackled on his fingertips.

Sarada had a sudden thought. If bolts were going to stand out in the darkness of a blackout, then they would just have to make sure it wasn't dark.

"Wait! I just had a good idea!" Sarada checked Mitsuki and turned her shuriken toward the stage.

Following her eyes, Mitsuki guessed her strategy and nodded. "A momentary opening, hm?"

"It's almost too easy compared with Dad's training."

The spotlight on top of the stage. If she could turn it toward the audience, she could dazzle the eyes of everyone in the place for a second or two.

She threw two shuriken in quick succession. They spun through the air. Four ropes held the massive spotlight in place at precisely the height of the second-floor seats. Her blades neatly severed the two ropes in front. The light lurched forward to shine on the crowd below.

"Huh? What's going on?!"

"It's so bright!"

The audience turned their faces away, dazzled.

In that opening, Mitsuki stretched out his arms toward the man on top of the dome. "Here we go, Sarada!"

The current shot forward from his hands, blending in with the light of the spotlight. Aiming for the center of these two parallel bolts, Sarada threw a kunai with everything she had.

Please! With a feeling like a prayer, she watched the blade race through the air. The brown tip headed for the space between the two currents as if sucked in by them.

Skweenk!

The force of the magnetic field sent the kunai streaking up into the roof to knock the sniper's rifle flying. The sniper lost his balance and toppled over.

"We got him."

It was a sink-or-swim strategy, but it had worked! Sarada and Mitsuki slapped their hands together in a high five.

✖ ✖ ✖ ✖ ✖

Meanwhile, on stage, stagehands raced up onto the catwalk to frantically retie the ropes that had inexplicably snapped in the middle of the show.

Even during this series of accidents, Boruto kept dancing, a true professional. The current song was a ballad, and he pretended to sing passionately, making great use of his fists. He guessed that Sarada and Mitsuki were responsible for the light. *What are they even doing? Of all times, right when I'm in the middle of the best part of the song...*

The people in the audience had also gotten used to the dazzling light at this point and listened quietly to the moving song, shielding their eyes with their hands.

Love is sweet chocolate ♪

If it's love, you and sweetie ♪

The lyrics, as always, described curious and whimsical worlds, but set to the gentle melody, they started to sound strangely ballad-like in their own special way.

"Boruto, that's great! Please keep it up. Walk gently to the front of the stage!"

Boruto moved toward the front just as Lily instructed, and the front row shrieked and waved their hands at him. Countless pink lightsticks flickered and shone in the crowd. The song was coming to its end. Once this ballad was over, they'd do a one-eighty and bring out a big dance number.

Snap.

He suddenly heard a pop in his ear, and then something very weird happened: his arms began to move on their own.

What the—?!

His arms steadily moved up toward the ceiling despite the fact that he wanted them to do something entirely different. The microphone fell to the ground with a dull thud, causing a burst of ear-splitting feedback.

If the audience found out he wasn't the real Lily, they would riot, and the TV cameras would catch the moment for posterity. He focused everything he had on pushing his arms back down. His muscles trembled from the strain.

What's going on? Some kind of genjutsu?!

Lily's voice continued to sing at the same loud volume despite the fact that he had dropped the mic. The fans began to murmur worriedly.

As Boruto started to panic, the pink nails on his fingertips shimmered.

No! He refocused the chakra in his body, and his hand temporarily turned back into Lily's. A moment later, the costume disappeared again. *What is even happening?!*

His body was trying to undo his transformation technique despite his own intentions. The chakra that was giving the order to undo the jutsu and the chakra that was giving the order to continue it—these two contradictory forces appeared to be fighting in the same arm. His hand changed back and forth from Lily's to his, blinking like a signal light.

"What? Huh? What's happening to Lily?"

"Hey, is this maybe a hologram performance?"

You gotta calm down and get this jutsu under control, Boruto told himself desperately. He tried to move his inexplicably restrained body.

His ankles gave out under him. The heels fell off and Boruto collapsed onto the stage. His feet were also turning back. The color drained from his face. He'd lost his balance because his feet had gotten smaller and the stiletto heels had come off.

Finally, in front of fifty thousand fans, his face began to spasm. It had only been an hour since he'd turned into Lily. Normally, it was easy for him to maintain a transformation for that length of time—longer, even. And yet her face shuddered and was replaced with his own. His entire body began to shrink.

It was all over. The jutsu was fading.

Ponk! His body was wrapped in smoke, and the transformation jutsu was released. He was Boruto once more.

"Huh? What happened to Lily?" The audience strained their eyes to get a better look at the stage.

All at once, something enveloped the area around him—a wall of water, as high as he was tall, surrounding Boruto like a cage.

What is this? What's going on?

He realized that his body was his to move again. He didn't get it, but he wasn't about to waste this chance. Hurriedly, he wove the signs to restore his Lily form.

The blasting music stopped abruptly and the dome fell silent. He could see a human shadow on the other side of the water wall. The shadow squatted down and picked something up. And then Boruto heard the thunk of the mic being turned on, and he realized the shadow had picked up the microphone.

"Show's over." The voice was emotionless and carried well, nothing like Lily's high-pitched voice. "All of you, leave immediately. Anyone acting suspiciously will be arrested."

"What is…Old Man Sasuke doing here?" Boruto shuddered, staring at the blurry shadow on the other side of his water prison.

Naturally, the audience revolted at this order.

"What the hell?! You gotta be kidding!"

"You a ninja?! Let Lily go!"

"Keep the show going!"

Boruto heard Sasuke sigh in annoyance.

Suddenly, Boruto felt a frightening amount of chakra surge forth, and a chill ran up his spine. A hair-raising purple giant sprouted up to block out the dome's ceiling. The warrior, clad in a traditional battle surcoat, held a massive bow. Its stern, golden eyes glittered fiercely, demonically.

"If you don't want to die, you will leave the dome. Right now. Every last one of you."

A terrified silence descended on the crowd. In the next instant, the members of the audience scrambled from the venue, screaming.

✖ ✖ ✖ ✖ ✖

After chasing out fifty thousand unarmed civilians by threatening them with Susano'o, Sasuke whirled around, thrust a hand through the water wall, and grabbed Boruto's shoulder. "About time for you to go back to your usual self, Boruto."

Poof!

The transformation jutsu was released the instant Sasuke's fingers touched him. He should have still looked like Himeno Lily, but in the blink of an eye, he was Boruto again.

The wall of water fell away, and Boruto stared in utter

confusion, unable to absorb even the first detail about what was happening.

"Where's the real Himeno Lily?" Sasuke asked him, his face expressionless.

"Oh! She's just over—huh?" Boruto pointed into the wings, but there was no sign of Lily there. He craned his neck searching for her, while beside him, Sasuke activated his Sharingan.

"Escaped up, hm?" he muttered, before turning toward the catwalk above the stage and throwing a shuriken.

"Aaaah!" Lily came falling down and Sasuke caught her midair by the arm. "Hey, what're you doing?! You could've for real hurt me, you know?!"

"So that was you then." Sasuke nodded

Huh? Boruto blinked rapidly and looked from Sasuke and back to Lily again. *Do they...know each other?*

CHAPTER 3

SASUKE'S STORY: STAR PUPIL

Once the audience and staff had been chased out, the dome was left a deserted shell. Boruto finally rejoined Sarada and Mitsuki in the green room. Lily had been made to sit on a folding chair in the center of the room, ankles tied to its legs with rope.

The fact that Sasuke had arrested Lily meant she was a suspect in some crime.

"What is this even about?! I don't get it! I wanna call my lawyer!"

The sight of Lily screaming and thrashing dumbfounded Boruto. "Lily... You're like a totally different person."

"You're holding me illegally! Am I supposed to be on my best behavior now?!" Lily shook the chair in anger.

"That's the same tone you had when we met before." Sasuke looked down on her like a scholar observing an animal. "Is this the real you then?"

"Old Man Sasuke," Boruto said, hesitantly. "You know Lily?"

"Mm." Sasuke continued to stare at the idol, who had turned

her face away, sulking. "We met once before. In the Thunder Train when the explosion happened."

"Huh?" Sarada furrowed her brow, doubtfully. "So then… she just happened to be on the train?"

"No. It's quite likely this woman is the ringleader's ally." Sasuke grabbed Lily's golden hair and pulled hard. Boruto gaped, jaw nearly hitting the floor when her entire head was yanked off and fell to the ground. Only upon closer inspection did he realize it had only been a wig that Sasuke had yanked off.

The real hair hidden beneath the long golden tresses was short and reddish brown.

"You can't talk your way out of this." Sasuke tugged hard on Lily's earlobe, where five pierced holes were neatly lined up.

"That's the same as the crew that attacked the train," Sarada muttered in surprise.

Lily bit her lip and said nothing.

"Five piercings. This is proof of Shigetsukyodan membership," Sasuke said.

"Shigetsukyodan?" Boruto raised a curious eyebrow. He'd never heard the word before.

"There's an outlying island in the western part of Shigetsu, the Land of Water. The community there has a tremendous amount of power," Sasuke explained dispassionately. "This midsize island, with a population of three thousand people, has long despised the Mizukage's rule and maintained a semi-isolation. Ten percent of the islanders on Shigetsu belong to the Shigetsukyodan. Their dogma controls large parts of everyday life there."

"Dogma?" Sarada asked.

"The worship of nature. What animates them is not the Mizukage but Mother Nature. They do not obey the

Mizukage. Or rather, that's been their stance for many years, but recently, the Mizukage's reconciliation policies have met with success, and diplomatic relations have gradually been warming up. Last year, the island was officially recognized by all as part of the Land of Water. But some very devout Shigetsukyodan members remain strongly opposed to the policy of opening the country up."

"So that faction turned to extremist attacks?" Mitsuki quickly realized the flaw in his theory. "But that doesn't make sense. Why would they target the Land of Fire and not the Land of Water?"

"Because the Hokage's efforts to develop Konoha are a large part of the reason the island is opening up. The desire to live in a wealthy society is what brought the island of Shigetsu out of isolation. This group of extremists is resentful of this, without any actual justification. The annoying part of all this is the fact that the leader of the Shigetsukyodan, their so-called 'holy master,' is personally giving the extremists orders. And..."

Sasuke looked down on Lily once again. "You're the holy master's only daughter, yes?"

"Lily's *what*?!" Boruto let out a wild cry as Sarada and Mitsuki looked at each other.

"There's no mistake," Sasuke declared. "I went to Shigetsu to confirm it. I never imagined you three would accept a mission from her, though... At any rate, the piercings in this ear are incontrovertible proof that this girl is a member of Shigetsukyodan."

"So what?" Lily snapped in a hard voice. She glared up at Sasuke. "I am indeed a member of Shigetsukyodan. And I also acknowledge that my father is the leader known as the holy master. But that's got nothing to do with me. I hate that close-minded, rural island. I fled to the Land of Fire because I wanted to be an idol in the city!"

Sasuke narrowed his eyes coldly. "So you're saying you didn't slip into the Land of Fire with the intention of spying?"

"I didn't! I hate my dad and all his friends, obsessed with that old way of thinking. I just wanted to be an idol."

"It's true." Boruto stepped in between Lily and Sasuke. "There's no way Lily's a bad guy."

Sasuke glanced wordlessly at Boruto and then turned back to Lily. "We'll go with a warning for now. I've already obtained a fair bit of information on you, so I'll know if you lie to me. You're going to answer some questions now."

"There's no reason for you to arrest me, you know!" Lily snarled. "You're the ones who'll be in trouble if you hurt me, like, okay? I've got a ton of lovely soul mates and all these memorial memories we've built up together. Don't underestimate our love connection!"

It was plain from the look on Sasuke's face that he had no idea what she was talking about.

"The lovely soul mates are her fans," Boruto quietly explained. "And the memorial memories are the times she's shared with her fans. The love connection is the bond they have with her."

Sasuke took a moment to digest this. "At any rate. You'll be under shinobi monitoring from now on."

"Uh? You mean arrest, right? I'm innocent," Lily said. "My fans won't just stand by quietly, you know. They'll come after you hard!"

"Do you think I care about that?"

"You might not, but what about the Hokage?"

The look on Sasuke's face changed at the mention of the Hokage.

Lily smiled. "The way the Hokage works, everyone's always watching him. A shinobi under the orders of the Hokage illegally restraining an innocent idol—you don't think that'd cause a scandal? I have tons of people watching my back, you know." Her tone was challenging.

"Let's start with the questions." Sasuke was unperturbed. "What's your objective in coming to this country?"

Lily clucked her tongue before responding reluctantly. "I left my hometown because I wanted to be an idol. The islanders are forbidden from leaving Shigetsu, so I boarded a ship in secret and fled."

"When was this?"

"Three years ago. Right around the time when more and more islanders were wanting to open up to the outside world, and the extremist Shigetsukyodan was starting to fight back."

"What is your current connection with the extremist faction?"

"I don't have one. I left them all a long time ago. About the only contact I've had with them is when they warned me about the assassination attempt."

"So then you did realize the letter was from them," Sasuke said.

"Well, you know. I figured they'd find out where I was once I got famous," Lily replied smoothly.

Sasuke carefully searched her face. "What reason do they have to hate you?"

"I guess because I abandoned the group and came to the Land of Fire to become an idol. They hate this place, and they never forgive traitors. I know they'll come for me again. But we can use that against them." Lily looked up at Sasuke with her large, round eyes. "I'll be the bait. The Shigetsukyodan extremists hate me for leaving the island and pandering to the Land of Fire. They'll for sure try and kill me again. I can be the bait that lures them in."

"An admirable proposal. But there's still one important question remaining," Sasuke said. "Where's your father?"

Lily visibly paled. Obviously upset, she lowered her eyes.

"You're very quiet all of a sudden. You said you had nothing
to do with them. In that case, why didn't you go to the Hokage for protection when you got the warning about the assassination attempt instead of reaching out to Boruto and his team?"

"That's…" She bit her lip. "It'd be bad for my image if people found out I was connected with that group. And I hated the idea of the concert being cancelled."

"Wasn't that letter actually a fake? Weren't you lying to Boruto and his team?"

"No!" Lily's head bounced up and her voice shook. "No. I've got nothing to do with my father."

"Then give me something on him."

Confronted with Sasuke's fathomless black eyes, Lily trembled and turned away.

"Do you have any idea where he might be?"

Lily pursed her lips together and looked down.

"Why won't you tell me?" Sasuke asked quietly. "If you truly don't get along with your father, why cover for him?"

Silence descended on the room. Lily held her tongue and swallowed back her words.

"If you're not going to tell me voluntarily…I don't want to do it, but my only choice is to force you to spit it out." Sasuke was about to activate the Sharingan when a hand reached out to grab his wrist.

"Just stop already," Sarada said. "Dad, Lily's not going to tell you. No way."

"Her father is trying to kill her because she rebelled against him and left their island. What reason could she possibly have to not tell me everything she knows about him?"

"She has a great reason," she said impatiently. "They're family."

Family. The word was unexpected. Sasuke blinked, caught off guard.

"No matter how much of a criminal he might be, there's no way a daughter's gonna sell out her dad. If I was in Lily's position, I wouldn't tell anyone about you, Dad. We're family," She said it as if it were the most obvious thing in the world.

The face of Sasuke's brother flashed through his head. His brother, who had spared Sasuke even though Danzo had ordered him to eliminate the entire clan. His brother, who had made Sasuke kill him in the end. Itachi, the kindest man Sasuke had ever known, had sacrified himself so that his brother could live. The choice was so desperate Sasuke had a hard time believing his brother had even made it, given how smart he was, how loyal to the mission.

Because they were family. His older brother had once taught him this, and now his daughter was reinforcing the lesson.

Sasuke glanced over at Boruto. He looked to be on tenterhooks, anxious as he watched Sarada and Sasuke. Naruto always used to look the same way with Sasuke.

He let out a short sigh. "I'll recognize your right to silence. But that doesn't mean you're cleared of suspicion. Until this is settled, you'll be under house arrest."

Lily clucked her tongue and looked away, annoyed. The gesture was rude, entirely at odds with her idol persona.

The newspaper headlines the following morning were bad.

Himeno Lily concert canceled. Audience in chaos.

Uchiha Sasuke cancels concert. Hokage's orders?

The articles criticized Sasuke, and every single one insisted on the need for an explanation as to why the concert had been cancelled. The stress her fans felt from not knowing what had happened that night, combined with Himeno Lily's disappearance after her abrupt announcement that she was stepping back from life in the public eye, turned into a burning anger that led to a week-long pile on.

Boruto could hardly stand it. He was outraged that the villagers would so quickly hang a ninja who had put his life on the line to keep them safe out to dry.

It had been three days since the start of the outrage machine. Their only word from Sasuke was a brief message: "Stand by until you hear from me."

Boruto, Sarada, and Mitsuki wandered aimlessly around the new town, unable to focus on their training.

"Dad won't tell me anything. I wanna talk to Old Man Sasuke." Boruto raised a heavy head. Before his eyes was a large video screen in the side of a building looking down on the intersection. An afternoon talk show was playing, one Naruto and Boruto had both been on before.

The guest that day was the man currently shaking the world up: Uchiha Sasuke. He was always so insistent on carrying out his work in the shadows, so the fact that he was appearing on a daytime talk show was unprecedented. Everyone whispered and wondered, certain that he would explain away the recent events to escape the recent barrage of criticism.

"So you're saying the Lord Hokage had absolutely nothing to do with the current situation with Himeno Lily?" asked the host.

"I acted alone." Sasuke's reply was brief, simple, straightforward. Every one of his replies was crystal clear, as he unwaveringly maintained that he was responsible for his actions, no matter what angle the host came at him from.

Was he trying to keep the fire from spreading to the

Hokage by using himself as a shield? Boruto glared up at the large screen in frustration.

"Himeno Lily hasn't been seen in public since the commotion, which has a lot of fans worried. Did you know that?"

"I can't answer questions about Himeno Lily herself. This matter is classified by the village."

"Some people are saying that you went too far by cancelling the concert."

"There was a risk of danger to the village. It had to be done."

"It had to be done? It's that sort of vagueness that Lily fans are likely to get upset about."

"It's the truth." Having said his piece, Sasuke abruptly ended the interview. He stood up and walked off screen.

"Oh! Umm. That's our show for today." The host quickly pulled herself together to end the program.

"Why won't you just tell them?" Boruto muttered bitterly.

"It was a mistake in our judgement," Mitsuki said in agreement. "When Lily came to us, we should've reported to the Lord Seventh instead of accepting the job."

"Aah," Boruto sighed. He was the one who had said they should take the job even though Mitsuki and Sarada had been against it. He'd wanted to succeed in the mission and get Sasuke's approval, but it had turned out exactly backwards. He'd only made trouble for Sasuke. He turned a gloomy face on Sarada. "Old Man Sasuke hasn't been home at all?"

Sarada shook her head. "He's been gone this whole time. Mom's not worried at all. She keeps saying he'll be fine."

Boruto looked up at the large screen resentfully. The camera was showing Sasuke's face in profile as he was on his way out of the studio.

"Whoa! It's Uchiha Sasuke!" A young man passing by said, eyes fixed on the screen.

The man with him frowned. "Uchiha Sasuke's so annoying. I mean, everyone was so excited about that concert and he just goes and cancels it. Just 'cause he's kinda hot doesn't mean he can do whatever he wants!"

Boruto was about to chase after the sneering men, but Mitsuki caught him by the arm and he pitched forward.

"What're you doin', Mitsuki?! Let me go!"

"If I let go, you're going to go punch those guys."

"Of course I am!" Boruto yelled, but when Mitsuki stared hard at him, he dropped his arm in defeat. "Fine, dammit. The way they're talking, though… They don't even know a thing about it!"

"That's why you can't punch them. Calm yourself down," Sarada said, her voice excessively quiet, and glared at the men's backs as they walked away. "Dad wouldn't care what guys like that said to him. It bugs me, though."

✖ ✖ ✖ ✖ ✖

It was a week later when Boruto woke up to the sound of something beating against the window at three-thirty in the morning. A hawk was pecking at the glass, looking exceedingly grumpy.

When Boruto opened the window, the bird dropped a piece of paper onto the floor and flew off.

Four a.m. in front of Warehouse No. 3, Old town.

"Four?!" Boruto headed for his closet in a total panic to change out of his pajamas. It was so like Sasuke to use a hawk to send orders in this day and age. He had only half an hour until the clock struck four.

"That bird was wasting its sweet time somewhere!" Boruto complained as he stepped out of the house, leaving his sleeping family behind. It was still very dark out. The full moon sat

low in the sky, ready to sink to the bottom of the night at
any moment.

When he arrived at the address on the note, Mitsuki and
Sarada were already there. If her bedhead was any indication,
Sarada had been awoken abruptly as well. Mitsuki looked the
same as he always did.

"Where's Old Man Sasuke?" Boruto asked.

"You're all here then?" Sasuke appeared from the shadows
behind them. "Mission time. The Shigetsukyodan extremists
are on board a cargo ship that's leaving for the Land of Water
in an hour. It's very likely Lily's father, the holy master, is
with them. They're probably planning to regroup with their
comrades in the Land of Water. We won't get this chance
again. We arrest the entire group tonight." He turned on his
heel as if to declare their immediate departure.

"Wait a second!" Boruto hurriedly called out. "Old Man
Sasuke, you okay?"

"What do you mean?"

"The whole TV thing, the public pile on. Because of us…"
Boruto clenched his hands and lifted his face. "Sorry. This
whole thing was because we messed up."

"Don't apologize. It's nothing serious." For all it had taken
for Boruto to muster the courage to apologize, Sasuke brushed
it aside in a millisecond.

"But everyone's calling you names and criticizing you," he
insisted.

"Much better than having your names come out," Sasuke
replied. "Come on. We have to hurry to the port."

The look of gloom didn't leave Boruto's face. Sasuke let out
a small sigh.

"Boruto. Being hated is part of my job. It's nothing for you
to be upset about."

"Don't you hate it, though? You're working missions to

protect the village and then... those people just say whatever they want about you."

"I understand how you feel. A relative of mine was unjustly smeared once, and I was furious about it. But when it came my turn, I suddenly didn't care either way. It's a strange thing. And...I don't really feel like I'm working to protect the village. If I had to say what my purpose is, it's helping your father." Sasuke tousled Boruto's blond hair. "So don't worry about it."

You say that, but... Boruto stared up at his teacher with a complicated mix of emotion. Sasuke's handsome countenance was as expressionless as ever. "Fine."

It wasn't as though he was actually persuaded by Sasuke's words, but he accepted the situation for the time being. After all, it was weird for him to be so worried when the man in question apparently couldn't have cared less.

Sasuke leaped up onto the roof of a house. He planned to take the rooftop route, taking advantage of the fact that there was no one around to see them. Boruto and his teammates followed suit, and the four of them jumped from house to house in a direct line for the port.

"Boruto, something is bothering me," Sasuke said. "You were attacked by the enemy on stage."

"Huh?"

"When I surrounded you in the Water Style wall."

Oh, right. So much had happened after the initial commotion that he'd forgotten, but it was true that immediately before Sasuke had shown up, he'd suddenly lost control of his body. His hands had moved on their own and for some reason released the transformation jutsu.

Boruto explained what happened, and Sasuke muttered, "The power to rob a target of free movement... It has to be Lightning Style."

"How do you know?" Mitsuki looked back curiously.

"You do know that when a person moves their body, orders from the brain become electrical signals and cause the muscles to move, yes?" Sasuke asked.

Sarada, Mitsuki, and Boruto assented in turn.

"It's just a hypothesis," their teacher continued. "But the enemy is most likely able to create a current that resembles the electrical signal from the brain. By sending that current into a target's body, they can feign an order from the brain and take over. Move your arms, undo the transformation jutsu, things like that."

"You mean they can produce a bioelectric current? Is that possible?" Sarada asked, looking as though she couldn't believe it.

"Mm." Sasuke nodded. "It would take incredibly fine control, but in theory, it's possible."

"So then…" Boruto looked at his own body, slightly creeped out. "The current the enemy created was flowing through me?"

"The fact that control was released the instant you were surrounded by the Water Style wall is proof. The enemy was sending electrical signals and controlling you from somewhere in the venue. The signal was interrupted when the wall of water encircled you completely."

Boruto cocked his head to one side. "Doesn't water conduct electricity really well, though?"

"Normally, water contains a lot of impurities," Sasuke told him. "Water conducts electricity well because those impurities act as bridges. But my Water Style contains zero impurities. It's pure water, composed only of oxygen and hydrogen."

Right. Water's made up of oxygen and hydrogen. Boruto remembered this from one of Shino's lessons at the academy.

"There's no impurities, so your water doesn't conduct electricity," Mitsuki said, as if all the pieces were falling into place.

"But being able to produce Lightning Style that mimics a bioelectric current," Sarada muttered, looking troubled. "That's a real threat."

"That's exactly right," Sasuke agreed. "You'd need to generate an electrical current so weak the target can't feel it when it enters the body. It's probably harder to maintain this kind of fine control with Lightning Style than it is to generate bolts of lightning."

Fine power control. Boruto had come face-to-face with that difficult task when they'd trained to roll doubles with their sugar-cube dice.

Sarada added another question to the pile. "Does the fact that they're using Lightning Style mean the enemies are ninja? The guys at the concert had guns."

"A limited number of them appear to use ninjutsu. The other fighters aren't shinobi, strictly speaking," Sasuke replied. "Shigetsukyodan is said to have originated when a faction of ninjas came to live in that remote area. Shigetsukyodan combatants likely have physical abilities on par with genin up to chunin. They differ from ninjas in that the majority of them rely on technology rather than chakra."

The party slipped out of the urban area and into the outskirts of the village. The scattered houses became fewer and farther in between, and their footholds changed from roof tiles to tree branches. Birds flew from the trees off into the sky, surprised by the force of their approach.

"Just as ninja use chakra and the power of the natural world, they observe nature and learn its truth in order to obtain its strength. That's science. Their high-performance explosives and guns are also byproducts of technological development. Science, ninjutsu, Shigetsukyodan—rather than running counter to each other, you could say that these three actually have the same roots."

Science and ninjutsu have the same roots? Boruto clenched his hands as he ran. He dropped his gaze to his feet. He'd thought science was in opposition to ninjutsu, that it was uncool and unfair. He still thought that to some degree even now. But he knew that Sasuke had expanded the scope of his ninja abilities by incorporating into his ninjutsu the truths of this world laid bare by science. He wanted to do that, too. He wanted to be a strong ninja like Sasuke.

"I can see it." Sasuke running in the lead said. "There's the boat."

The forest opened up to reveal the inky void of the ocean spread out before them. The boat docked in the tiny harbor was so massive it dwarfed the port. Painted navy and brown, it floated there, a dirty shadow against the moonlight. Boruto strained his ears. Above their footfalls, he heard the faint sound of the waves scratching against the surface. The enemy was in the belly of that ship.

They ran faster.

CHAPTER 4

SASUKE'S STORY: STAR PUPIL

4

A dozen or so members of the cargo ship crew were lined up neatly on the dock, waiting for Sasuke and his students. A man looking slightly more polished than the others—presumably the captain—stepped forward. "The Lord Hokage has informed us of the situation. We've set the ship's controls as arranged to set sail in ten minutes. It's on full autopilot until the ship reaches the port in the Land of Water."

"There's no crew left on board?" Sasuke asked.

"No, this is everyone."

"So then the only people in the boat are those guys?" Boruto said, surprised.

"Mm." Sasuke nodded. "We couldn't risk having the crew caught up in the fighting, so we had them disembark before the ship pulls out."

"So they're like rats in a trap then," Mitsuki murmured, looking up at the massive boat.

Sasuke had apparently prepared for just about everything in the brief window before the ship sailed.

According to the captain, the cargo ship was the maximum

allowable size, spanning a total of eighty meters and weighing 1,600 tons. The drawbridge-style door to the rear created a small wharf when opened, allowing two jet skis to be ridden out onto the water to test water quality or in times of emergency. The interior was divided into three levels, and the only way to move between levels was to use the staircase out front or the central stairs.

"The fact that the stairs are the only way in and out makes going after them pretty easy, but sneaking in gets a lot more challenging. You're basically totally exposed." Mitsuki frowned.

"We can just go in another way," Sasuke said, and pointed to the center of the ship.

Following his finger, Boruto saw round windows on what looked to be the ship's second level. They could hide by those windows after the ship pulled out until they saw their chance and then break the windows to slip inside—that was the plan, apparently.

Carefully cloaking their chakra, Sasuke and his team clambered up the outside of the boat and glued themselves to the window area. Peering inside, Boruto saw a simple bed and a small desk inside the gloomy room. There was no sign of Shigetsukyodan.

"We go in through here once we pull out of the port," Sasuke instructed, and the team nodded.

The ship was set to sail at five a.m. They held their breath in the predawn gloom and waited for the moment to come.

"Four, three, two..." Sarada counted down, looking at her watch. "...one, zero!"

At precisely five o'clock, a dull horn sounded, and the ship slowly pulled away from shore.

After confirming that the port was receding, Boruto turned toward the window and raised a fist. "'Bout time to break the glass?"

"No, there's no need for that." Sasuke said. He touched his hand to the window. In an instant, the glass melted away like water.

"Whoa!" Boruto's feet slipped in his surprise, and Sasuke caught him to stop him from plunging down into the water. He lifted his elbow and popped Boruto through the empty window frame to the inside of the ship.

"How'd you do that?!" Boruto's eyes were wide with admiration.

"I caused a highly compressed Fire Style heat to instantly spread across the glass and melt it," Sasuke said, stepping through the window frame. Sarada and Mitsuki followed.

Sasuke started to activate his Sharingan to discover the enemy's position, and then stopped. He looked back at Sarada. "Sarada, can you search the ship with your Sharingan?"

"Huh?" His daughter was surprised by the question. "Yeah. But are you sure you want me to do it, Dad? This ship's pretty big. It might be better if you—"

"You'll be fine. Go ahead and try."

This is actual battle, a valuable experience, ideal for helping my students grow, Sasuke thought. He remembered their fight with Momoshiki. Instead of hammering down with a Rasengan blow himself, Naruto had gotten Boruto to do it. At the time, Sasuke had questioned why Naruto would go out of his way to hand the final strike to another, but now it made perfect sense. Naruto had wanted to give his son experience in an actual fight.

Sarada closed her eyes. When her lids flew up again, the Sharingan had been activated. A red light shone in her irises, three dark magatama shapes floating up in them.

"There's a total of three groups," she said. "Four people on the deck, four behind the central stairs on the second level, and one in the far west on the third level. And...they've laid explosives."

"Explosives?!" Boruto shouted, eyes opening wide.
"Where? How many?"

"All over. A lot."

He drew a breath in through his teeth. "Seriously?"

Sasuke closed his eyes and quietly activated his own Sharingan to confirm that Sarada's conclusions were accurate. The explosives were in a total of eighteen locations. They looked to be set off by timers rather than proximity.

"From here, we each move on our own," Sasuke announced, and his students stared with wide eyes.

"What? You mean we'll be separated?" Mitsuki asked.

Sasuke nodded. "Boruto, you take the third level. Sarada, second. Mitsuki, head for the deck. Don't challenge them directly. Aim for a surprise attack and render them helpless. And don't damage the boat if you can help it."

"What about you, Old Man Sasuke?"

"I'll collect the explosives."

Mitsuki and Boruto glanced at each other, half-anxious, half-excited. Sarada, eyes lowered, looked much less confident.

"You seem anxious, Sarada," Sasuke said.

"To be honest, I'm kinda worried," Sarada confessed haltingly. "When Mitsuki and I chased down those guys in the audience at Lily's concert, the man in the ceiling didn't hesitate to kill them to shut them up even though they were his own comrades. I don't know if I'm really ready to take on a group with that kind of mindset all by myself."

"That kind of mindset?" Sasuke chuckled. "That mindset is precisely what limits them. Anyone who doesn't value their comrades is garbage." The words were those of his former teacher. A long time had passed since his young ninja days, but Kakashi continued to be Sasuke's master even now.

Sarada looked even more uncertain. Sasuke set the palm of

his hand down on her head. "Don't look like that. I'd never let my comrades be killed."

He had the sudden realization that he was now passing down to the children of the next generation words that had been given to him so long ago. It was a strange feeling, like he'd extended his own life somehow, like everything he'd worked to protect was coming full circle as he passed the torch he'd received as a child himself from the adults around him.

"Yeah. I'm feeling like I'll be okay now. I'll fight hard, Dad." Sarada said, looking up from under her father's large hand.

"Mmm. And take this." Sasuke fastened a small wristband machine onto Sarada's wrist. The top of the device had a small opening to launch the scrolls inside.

"Dad, this is…"

A scientific ninja tool, a revolutionary invention that allowed someone other than the weaver of a jutsu to use it by sealing the ninjutsu into a small scroll. It was the cutting edge of ninja tools created by the scientific ninja team, the pride of the village of Konoha.

�֎ ✖ ✖ ✖ ✖

Mitsuki climbed the outer wall of the ship and looked out at the deck from the cover of the railing. This wasn't a passenger ship, so the deck was small and visibility was poor. He saw no sign of anyone moving, but he could hear whispered voices in conversation. He climbed up onto the wooden flooring and moved from shadow to shadow until he spotted several men crouching behind the line of lifeboats. Four in total. They appeared to be doing something with the square devices that surrounded them.

Explosives.

He decided it was best to disarm the explosives first, even if it meant letting some of the men get away. Cloaking himself in darkness, Mitsuki crept slowly toward the men. He stretched out an arm and reached toward the devices the men crowded around.

"Hey! What's this?!"

By the time one of the men noticed his arm and raised a voice in alarm, Mitsuki was already grabbing the square box and shrinking his arm back toward his body. He took a look at the device he'd recovered.

"What? This is it?"

The acrylic box was empty, still waiting to be filled with explosive material. He tossed it onto the deck and kicked at the wood beneath his feet.

Two of the men held up guns while the other two tried to flee into the belly of the ship.

Two gunshots rang out, but neither bullet so much as grazed Mitsuki.

He closed the distance between them in an instant and grabbed the man on the right by the neck to slam his head into the face of the man on the left. The fierce collision made a dull *whuck* sound, and the man who'd been headbutted swooned and collapsed. The other one was still ready for action, and he grabbed Mitsuki's wrist to try and peel his hand away from his neck. Mitsuki slammed his head into the wall.

"Gah!" The man let out a brief cry as Mitsuki slowly tightened his grip, applying pressure to his carotid artery. His face turned a blue-black and saliva spilled out of a corner of his mouth. The scrabbling hand dropped down to hang limply at his side. The whole process took seven seconds. When Mitsuki released his hand, the man slid to the ground, unconscious.

Good. That's two of them out of the way. Mitsuki breathed a sigh of relief, but the moment was fleeting.

The sudden roar of an engine echoed across the ocean. He

raced over to the railing and leaned over to look toward the rear of the ship. The two men who had fled were escaping on the jet skis.

"This is bad!" Mitsuki leaped over the railing and dropped toward the ocean surface twenty meters below. Just before he hit the water, he kicked at the ship to send himself shooting out to one side. He reached toward the jet ski with everything he had. His fingertips just barely latched onto the rear of the fleeing machine.

"Dammit! Let go!" The rider veered wildly from side to side, trying to shake Mitsuki loose. Powerful jets of water shot out of the nozzles right at Mitsuki, but he maintained his grip. He contracted his arm to slide along the water surface and jump onto the seat of the jet ski.

"You—!" The man looked back and turned his gun on him, but they were too close together. Mitsuki grabbed the gun with his bare hands and turned it to the sky. The gun fired and Mitsuki used the recoil to yank the weapon up and slammed the grip into the back of the man's head.

"Aah!" He lurched forward, and Mitsuki followed up with a knee strike. The man's eyes rolled back in his head as he lost consciousness.

"That's one..." Moving the unconscious man to his feet, Mitsuki grabbed the handlebars and yanked on the throttle.

The engine roared, and working at top speed, the jet pump beneath the seat pushed the jet ski to maximum speed in the blink of an eye. Spray shooting up around him, Mitsuki raced after the man fleeing ahead of him, but he couldn't manage to close the distance between the two machines. The jet skis were both capable of the same performance and were both running at full throttle.

I'm not going to get anywhere like this. If he would just slow down a tiny bit...

Frustrated, Mitsuki noticed a small button just below and to the right of the handlebars. An orange diode shone in the square button, and below it, the word *ignition*. The button that turned the engine off and on. If he pushed it, the jet ski would immediately decelerate.

He looked ahead at the man he was chasing. His jet ski had the same button, and he was just five meters ahead of Mitsuki, a distance his Wind Style could cover with ease. If he sent a breeze to push on the ignition switch of the other man's jet ski, he could catch up.

Mitsuki gripped the handlebars and considered. After a moment's hesitation, he made his decision. *It'll be okay. I know I can do it. The button's not as fragile as a sugar cube.*

At that moment, a slightly larger wave rolled in, and the machine bobbed up into the air.

Mitsuki gripped the seat tightly between his legs and stepped hard on the chest of the man stretched out at his feet so he wouldn't fall off. He reached out to launch a Wind Style attack at the candy-sized button. The gust twisted and roared as it flew toward the orange light. He couldn't see whether or not it hit the ignition switch.

A moment later, Mitsuki's jet ski crashed back onto the water surface. Instantly, he was opening up the throttle again. He cut through the pillar of water his landing had created and charged forward.

The jet ski in front was advancing with similar ferocity, but its speed was quickly dropping. The orange light of the switch was out.

Did I hit it? Mitsuki licked his dry lips.

Clearly perplexed, the man ahead of him yanked on his own throttle, but he kept slowing down. The distance between them was shrinking with every breath.

Just about within reach!

Mitsuki stretched out his arm as the man turned around. A look of shock rose up on his face, and his panic made his riding erratic. In the next instant, the jet ski pitched forward with incredible force. The man was launched high into the air. The jet ski kept going, skidding along the water surface and spinning three times. Black smoke erupted up from the engine. A second later, the machine exploded.

"Aah, give me a break!"

Mitsuki jumped up from his seat. Swinging his arm like a whip, he caught the man who had been tossed up like a rag doll and then whirled around in midair to slam a fist into the man's head to keep him quiet before dropping back down onto the jet ski. He laid the unconscious man at his feet on the opposite side of the first man and grabbed the handlebars.

Oof. That's my mission complete. Taking a breath, he loosened his grip on the throttle to slow the machine. But his speed showed no sign of changing.

"Huh?" He tried pushing the ignition switch.

Not only did the jet ski not stop, it didn't even slow.

"Is it maybe broken?"

Was it the impact with the water?

The machine should already have been going as fast as it could, but now its speed seemed to be gradually increasing. It was only a matter of time before he lost his balance and the jet ski toppled over. Each little bounce sent a stinging shock through his body. *If we flip over at this speed...* He could have saved himself any number of ways if he had been alone, but it would be a Herculean feat to also rescue his unconscious prisoners.

Up ahead, he noticed a large wave coming right for him.

"Th-this is not good..." He had no choice. If he could just keep these two alive and able to talk, his team would take care of the rest in the worst-case scenario.

Mitsuki pulled the two men in close and tucked them

under his arms. The wave was about to hit them and flip the jet ski over. The instant it did, he would jump up and fall backward onto the water. He'd just have to hope he would still be able to swim back to the ship after that, and to bring the men back with him. Bracing himself for impact, Mitsuki got ready to jump.

There was a sudden crack, and the jet ski abruptly slowed down.

"Huh?"

Crackle crackle.

It sounded like something crystallizing around him.

Decelerating in the blink of an eye, the jet ski slid over the tall wave and finally came to a stop. Cold air descended around them, even though they were out on the open water. His breath was coming out in white puffs. Mitsuki looked around incredulously.

"This…"

The ocean had frozen as if to embrace the jet ski. He looked back and saw an ice bridge stretching out from the prow of the ship in the distance.

"Is that…Sasuke?"

🗙 🗙 🗙 🗙 🗙

After sneaking down onto the third and lowest level, Boruto held his breath and examined his surroundings. The wooden floor was covered in enormous containers, each about two meters tall, making for poor visibility. On the other hand, the containers also meant there were plenty of places for him to hide.

According to Sarada, there was only one man on the third level. He was apparently walking around the containers on his own, which meant he might have been looking for something to steal or maybe places to lay more explosives.

Boruto spotted the shadow of a man crouching down in front of a container near the center of the room. He appeared to be alone, just as Sarada had seen with her Sharingan.

Behind a container, Boruto kneaded chakra in his palms. Up against just one enemy, his best option was to knock him unconscious with a Rasengan blast. But he needed to fine-tune the blast so that he didn't do anything more than knock the man out. Plus, the path between Boruto and his target was littered with heavy containers on both sides. He would have to carefully determine his trajectory to avoid hitting them.

He set his aim on the man's back and quietly slipped out of the shadow before launching a super-controlled version of his Rasengan to make sure he didn't accidentally kill the man.

Whr whd whd whd whd!

The Rasengan was supposed to silently whizz ahead and knock the man out, but instead, it sent a dozen or so of the containers flying, making a shocking amount of noise in the process. The blow hit the man squarely in the chest. As he collapsed, pieces of the destroyed containers rained down on him.

"Huh?! Why?!"

Boruto had been careful to adjust the amount of power he used, so why had the containers flown up? He was baffled for a moment, but then it all came together for him. He'd thought the containers were full, but they were actually empty. With nothing to weigh them down, the close-range Rasengan wind pressure had been more than they could take. He nodded in understanding just as a remarkably large container fragment fell on top of the man with a thud.

Ah, crap! Boruto raced over to the man splayed out on the floor and pushed the pieces of debris aside. He ripped off the purple fabric that covered the lower half of the man's face and brought his ear in close. He heaved a true sigh of relief when he could hear the regular in-out of the man's breath. "Great!"

"Tell me what exactly is great about this!" Sarada popped her head through a large hole in the ceiling.

"Sorry, my bad. My Rasengan was a little too strong." He kicked at the floor and jumped up through the hole to the second level.

"'My bad'?!" she snarled. "Your explosion helped my enemy get away!!"

"Look, I didn't mean to. How was I supposed to know the containers were empty?"

"That's because you're never think—"

Crackle crackle!

Lightning shot through the air between them, and the two ninja leapt for cover behind the containers.

"How many are there?" Boruto asked.

"Four!" Sarada snapped. "The one with the lightning's behind the door."

He met her eyes briefly before flying out from behind the container to charge toward the stairs and kick down the door. Wood fragments exploded outward, quickly followed by a Lightning Style unleashed on Boruto.

He dropped into a defensive posture and immediately guarded with a Water Style wall. But as long as the water wasn't pure, it was an excellent conductor, and naturally, the Lightning Style pierced his wall.

"Youch!"

A burning pain shot through his arm, and he staggered backward. The lightning user moved to close the distance between them.

Crap. The word had no sooner crossed his mind than the man's eyes were rolling back in his head. He sank down to the ground, revealing Sarada standing behind him. She'd apparently given the man a solid bop on the head.

"What were you even thinking, you idiot?! Of *course* electricity's gonna pass through Water Style!"

"I know that!"

Right. He did know that. But he'd had in his head that pure water wall of Sasuke's and had used Water Style without thinking.

Before he had time to reflect on this, a bullet ricocheted off the floor at his feet. He figured out the position of the sniper from how the bullet splintered the wood on the floor and headed for the right side of stairs.

He startled the man hiding behind the wall there, who reflexively fired his gun without aiming. The bullet shot through a container far behind him. Crouching low, Boruto charged. The man lowered the barrel of the gun and concentrated on putting Boruto in his sights.

Taking advantage of this opening, Sarada slipped around behind him and kicked the enemy in the back. "Take that!"

The man pitched forward in a crescent and the barrel rose back up. In an instant, Boruto was upon him, twisting his wrist toward the ceiling and forcing the gun from his grasp. The man let out a pained noise. Sarada grabbed his neck from behind and slowly tightened her grip. When the man dropped off into a gentle slumber, she laid him down on the floor and chased after Boruto, who was already off and running.

"Two more, yeah?" he asked.

"Should be." She nodded.

He'd heard an engine earlier, which meant someone was using the jet skis. No one would have been stupid enough to run to the lower deck, where there was no path of escape. They raced up the stairs and out onto the deck.

"Where the heck did they go?" Boruto whirled his head

around. There were no lights on the deck, but he could see the area around him well enough.

He heard the rustling of cloth and leaped backward at the same time as Sarada.

Bang!

A gunshot. He couldn't tell where it had come from, but Sarada instantly activated her Sharingan.

"Behind the lifeboat!"

"I got this!"

He concentrated his chakra in the soles of his feet and leaped directly upward. A target in vertical motion was half-impossible for a gun with no scope to get a lock on. The barrel wavered, its user unable to accurately measure the distance from his hiding place behind the boat. Boruto came down hard on the gun barrel and let his momentum propel him forward into the sniper's face, knocking the man unconscious.

In the next instant, a fiery pain blossomed in his shoulder. Bright red blood jetted up from the fresh bullet wound. Looking back, he spotted a man hiding behind the door pointing a gun straight at him. Boruto flung himself backward, but there turned out to be no need for that.

Sarada threw a shuriken to split the barrel of the handgun perfectly in two. "Take that!" she shouted, closing the distance between them to swing her right fist squarely at the man's face. He went flying onto a pile of inflatable rafts and didn't get up again.

Four. That was all of them.

"Boruto, your shoulder's bleeding!" Sarada came racing over to him.

"It's just a flesh wound," he told her, touching his shoulder gingerly.

"Well, we better stop the bleeding at any rate. I'm ripping

your shirt." She held up a kunai. He could feel that the wound wasn't serious, but he still nodded and moved his arm as if to take off his jacket.

Crackle. He heard something that sounded like a firecracker going off, and his body suddenly stiffened. Once again, he was gripped by the feeling that his own body wasn't his to control, just like at the concert.

Before he even had the chance to be upset at what was happening, his arms were reaching forward, ignoring the commands his own brain was sending out, to yank the kunai from Sarada's hand.

"Get back, Sarada!" Boruto barely managed to squeeze the cry out of his frozen throat.

"Boruto?!" She immediately jumped back. "What's wrong?!"

"Same as before… I…" That was all he could manage to say. Even the muscles in his face would no longer do what he told them to.

His feet kicked at the ground on their own. His zombie arm slashed the kunai at Sarada—once, twice. Sarada deftly avoided the blows, but she didn't look like she could hold out for long. With almost nothing on the deck for her to hide behind, she was at a severe disadvantage.

"Sarada!" he cried. "Punch me in the face! Knock me out!"

"I'd be happy to, if we knew I could free you like that!" Sarada shouted, a desperate edge in her voice. "But maybe you'll keep coming at me while you're unconscious! Like a zombie!" She kicked up a life preserver, and the plastic ring hit him in the face. His head spun and his face went numb, but his body kept moving, nimble as ever, despite the fact that he was on the verge of passing out.

His nose was bleeding, but without the ability to control his body, he couldn't even wipe it away.

Dammit. What am I gonna do here? The last time this had happened, he'd escaped thanks to the pure water of Sasuke's Water Style. He would just have to do the same thing.

If I just make a wall of pure water, then I can crush this.

"Who's controlling him?" Sarada shouted, her eyes racing around the deck. "Where are you?! Show yourself! Get out here!"

Boruto tried to knead chakra around his body, but his hopes were dashed. His body still wouldn't accept his control.

He took a deep breath and held it. He had to forget about what was going on. Forget everything—Sarada, his zombie body, the pain in his shoulder, all of it—and close himself off in his own head. He filled his mind with the image of cold water. Pure hydrogen and oxygen, just the two elements—

The kunai he held slammed down to stab deep into the deck. Bits of wood flew up into his cheeks.

Collecting his scattered focus, Boruto once more tried to concentrate on his chakra. He calmed his mind, leaned into the image of water.

His body slashed horizontally with the kunai. With exquisite reflexes, Sarada dodged the blow, and Boruto lost his balance. With no control over his body, a graceful fall was out of the question and he landed on his face. But even before the pain of this hit him, his body leaped to its feet again.

I can't concentrate. And anyway, why would I be able to make pure *water now when I've never done it before?*

Spirits sinking, he noticed his free hand digging into his pocket. "Sarada! Shuriken!"

A heartbeat later, his hand found the shuriken and flung it at Sarada. The shuriken raced through the air, spinning ferociously, and ripped into Sarada's shoulder.

"Ow!" Sarada screwed her face up as blood started to ooze from the wound.

Boruto's feet kicked at the deck, racing to take advantage of Sarada's momentary weakness with the kunai held high.

"Sarada! Run!" he cried.

The slicing blade glittered sharply. Sarada flew back to dodge the blow, but the tip of the kunai slid through the lock of hair hanging in front of her face, and it flopped down onto the deck. She stumbled and staggered as Boruto closed in on her, still brandishing the kunai.

"Run! Sarada!" Boruto cried, desperately.

Sarada grinned. "Not run, Boruto."

Huh?

He stared, baffled, as Sarada pressed a button on the scientific ninja tool on her wrist. A scroll popped out and she held it high above her head. Erupting from the center of the scroll was...

Water Style.

Water geysered up and rained down around them.

"Whoa!" Doused in the heavy water, Boruto pitched forward onto the deck.

He tried to get to his feet and realized he finally had control of his body back. Which meant this water...

"It's pure. Dad made it." Sarada smirked, similarly soaked. The scientific tool her father had given her when they were setting out had been equipped with a pure Water Style to escape the control of a bioelectrical attack.

Boruto leaped to his feet and stared hard at his wet hand. Pure water. A fusion of nothing but oxygen and hydrogen. He needed to remember its feel on his skin so he could make it himself. *I couldn't generate this under my own power now, but I will next time.*

He tensed his entire body. The enemy must have been able to see Sarada and Boruto in order to attack with the faint electrical current. It was very likely that they were being watched from somewhere nearby even now. He and Sarada stood back-to-back and scanned their surroundings. Several minutes passed with no movement from their opponent.

Did they run away?

He heard a faint noise, like gears biting into each other, and gasped. When he turned his head in the direction of the sound, the bench there exploded.

Dodging the pieces of wood flying through the air, Boruto and Sarada leaped backward, Boruto to the right, Sarada to the left. It wasn't a large explosion but it was enough to knock them off balance.

Bang! Bang!

The first bullet grazed Boruto's thigh. The second one hit his side. Whirling around, he saw the face of the person standing there, and all color drained from his own.

"Sorry, Boruto," said Lily.

"What are you…" His voice shook. "You… So you're one of the bad guys?!"

"Bad? Maybe to you." Lily's face was cold, hostile. The barrel of the gun in her hand was pointed directly at Boruto. The purple outfit she wore proved, whether he liked it or not, her membership in Shigetsukyodan.

He stood rooted to the spot, stunned, unable to accept the sight before him.

Sarada took a step forward. "Boruto trusted you. I won't let you get away with this!" she shouted, and threw a shuriken.

Instead of stepping aside, Lily swiftly held a hand up in front of her body, palm out, fingers pressed together, and straightened her back.

Sarada's shuriken should have plunged into her chest, but instead, the blade swerved wildly to one side just as it was about to hit Lily. Its once straight trajectory curving unnaturally and the blade stabbed into Lily's open palm.

"Huh?!" Shaken, Sarada immediately threw three more shuriken.

But the result was the same. The shuriken curved wildly along the way and were almost sucked into Lily's hand.

"I can't target critical points?" Sarada muttered and furrowed her brow.

Plasma crackled and popped around Lily's hand. Her palm was enveloped in in electricity. Which meant...

"She... Did she concentrate current in her hand to create a magnetic field?" Boruto wondered, stunned.

She had generated a magnetic field in her hand using an electrical current and avoided any critical hits by pulling in the metal shuriken and kunai. Boruto and Sarada wouldn't be able to do any real damage with long-distance shuriken attacks. It was indeed a desperate way of fighting.

"A close-range battle it is!" Boruto leaped at Lily.

She pulled all four shuriken out of her hand and launched them at him. They closed in from all directions, including his blind spot. It would be impossible to dodge them all. He braced himself for at least one hit, bending over to protect his heart and other vital organs.

Ting! Ting! The shuriken bounced back with a crisp sound. By the time he realized Sarada had knocked them down with an assist, Lily was already on top of him.

"Ngh!" He grabbed the barrel of her gun and yanked it upward just as she fired twice.

The recoil from the shots made the bones of his fingers tingle. Boruto pulled his arm back with everything he had, ready to rip the gun from her hands, but Lily didn't resist. Instead, she let go, causing him to lose his balance and pitch forward.

"Whoa?!"

Ready for this opening, Lily thrust a hand out to press

down on his chin and shove the long fingernail of her thumb into his mouth.

This is bad! He bit down as hard as he could on her thumb.

Not only did Lily not flinch, she smiled slightly. "If your body is covered in pure water…then I just have to release the current inside of it."

An intense, fiery shock shot through him. "Hngah!" Fireworks exploded before him, and his body reeled backwards. Every muscle in his body seized, and he shook almost hard enough to turn him inside out. His mind went white, and he desperately tried to hang onto his fading consciousness. He couldn't pass out now and leave Sarada to fight Lily on her own.

No way a shinobi's gonna lose to an idol in a fight!

Through sheer willpower, he raised a trembling hand and grabbed Lily's wrist. In is other hand, he kneaded chakra. *Rasengan.* But his muscles were still trembling uncontrollably. He wouldn't be able to fine-tune this blow, and if he hit her with a full-power Rasengan, Lily wouldn't survive.

"Hngh…" He groaned. He bent so far backward that his spine creaked. *I don't have time to hesitate. I just have to do this…*

"Take that!" Sarada landed a kick in Lily's side, and the idol's finger was yanked out of Boruto's mouth. The pop star's slender body flew helplessly through the air and somersaulted across the deck.

Freed from the electrical attack, Boruto got to his knees. Panting, he wiped the sweat away. The Rasengan he'd kneaded into existence disappeared with a faint *fwsh.*

"Boruto, you okay?!"

"Yeah, I can move…"

That Sarada, no mercy… She doesn't hold back against another woman.

His relief was fleeting. Once he got to his feet, his jacket suddenly puffed up. "Huh?"

The kunai in his pocket ripped through the fabric of his jacket and flew upward.

"Aah, dammit!" Boruto reached out, but his fingers grazed the kunai in vain.

The weapon shot toward Lily's bloody hand and dug into the center of it. A smile flitted across her face as she yanked it out and turned the tip not toward Boruto or Sarada but her own throat. She would kill herself before she would let herself be captured. Just like the other Shigetsukyodan members.

"Lily! Stop!" Even as he leaped at her, Boruto knew it was no use. He wasn't going to make it.

A black cloak flapped behind her. There was a flash of movement as something chopped down onto her wrist, and the kunai fell from her hand.

Sasuke kicked the blade into the ocean. "Slipped out of house arrest?"

Lily stiffened. Sasuke's tone was extremely even, but there was a hard edge to it that sent a shiver up Boruto's spine.

Lily had just barely managed to hold her own against Boruto and Sarada. Now that Sasuke had appeared, that difference in power would be overwhelming, an unbreachable gap. Even still, she turned bravely to glare at Sasuke.

"I'd rather die than be your prisoner." Her tone was challenging, but she no longer had any means to commit suicide. Not only had she used every weapon in her arsenal, she'd been restrained by Sasuke. She had no chance at victory.

"Lily..." Boruto's voice trembled. "Why would you..."

Lily frowned and said nothing. She dropped her head.

Boruto clenched his fists. *She taught me all kinds of idol stuff. I even maybe thought she was kinda great. But that was all just an act?!* It was all too much.

There was a sound from the prow of the ship. He turned

to see that the man who'd been stretched out on the rubber lifeboats had regained consciousness and was now pointing a broken handgun at them.

"Th-that guy... He's awake!" Boruto jumped at him.

But after failing to get off a surprise shot, the man realized he had no chance of victory now. He tossed the gun aside and pulled himself to his feet before spreading his arms and falling backward toward the sea.

"Wh—Another suicide?!"

"Boruto! Don't!"

Sasuke grabbed Boruto's shoulder to keep him from running over to the side of the ship.

Boom!

A pillar of water shot up and rocked the boat.

"Suicide bomb?!" Boruto looked up at his teacher. "He had a bomb on him?!"

"No." Sasuke shook his head. "Most likely, he launched a full-power Lightning Style technique in the ocean."

The issue now was that the explosion had been right beside the boat, and the ship's construction just happened to be weakest on its sides. A massive fissure ripped through the body of the enormous vessel. The weight of the ship being rocked back and forth by the surging waves only helped the breach grow.

The ship was splitting in half before their eyes.

"We're gonna sink!" Sarada shrieked.

"Don't panic," Sasuke said, calmly. "The size of this ship, it won't sink if we freeze the ocean."

"Huh?! Can you even do that, Dad?!"

A red shadow shot across Boruto's field of view. It was Lily, he realized, but she was already beyond his reach. Without a moment's hesitation, she jumped into the fissure between the crumbling planks of the deck.

"Lily!" Without thinking, Boruto leaped into the crumbling interior of the ship after her.

CHAPTER 5

SASUKE'S STORY: STAR PUPIL

The holy master said we'd go to heaven if we died for Shigetsukyodan. I wonder if I will. I've lived my whole life, all these years, caring for nothing but Shigetsukyodan. The holy master and the brethren hate me. They think I'm a traitor. But I was trying to do what's best for us all. I wonder if God will understand. Or will God send me to hell like the master would? Either way's fine. At any rate, I'll know soon enough.

When she opened her eyes and saw water cutting diagonally across the gloom before her, Lily understood that she was in neither heaven nor hell. It wasn't the water that was diagonal, but her, lying not on a bed but a wall. To her right, a broken fluorescent light on the ceiling was close enough for her to touch if she reached for it.

She had leaped into the sinking ship, and yet she had somehow managed to survive.

I know I have terrible luck, but this is ridiculous.

"You awake?"

"Ah!" Lily jumped at the sudden voice. She turned to see the cheery blue eyes of Uzumaki Boruto. The person she had lied to and taken advantage. "You saved me?"

"Yup," he replied casually. "Don't move too much. It could bring half the ship down on our heads."

She surveyed their surroundings. They appeared to be inside an air pocket in the upper part of the skewed cabin.

"The water level hasn't changed for a while, so we're maybe done sinking for now," Boruto said. "If we just sit tight, Old Man Sasuke'll come rescue us."

"You really trust him, huh?"

"He is my master, after all."

They fell silent again.

Lily bent her knees to sit in the small space between the water and the wall and stared absently at container fragments and chunks of wood. Next to her, Boruto was feigning indifference, but she knew he was watching her like a hawk. *Why did this kid rescue me?*

"Hey, why's it called Shigetsukyodan?" he asked, out of the blue.

"Huh?"

"I mean, the moon's usually silver, right? But *shigetsu* means 'purple moon.' How come?"

"Because that's how it looks," Lily replied, not looking at him. "In the fall, in the water around the island where I grew up, the plankton multiply all at once, and the sea turns this reddish color. When it does, the reflection of the moon in the water has this purple tinge to it. The purple full moon's so beautiful, shimmering on the surface of the sea, cloaked in white waves... Our ancestors saw the presence of God in it. That was the start of Shigetsukyodan."

She clamped her mouth shut. In her joy at being asked about her home, she'd let herself go into far too much detail.

"Wow! Is that what happened?" Boruto's admiration sounded so innocent. "Huh. So you guys like the night sky."

"What?" Lily frowned.

"Your piercings are like a constellation," he pointed out.

Saying nothing, she turned her palm upward and lowered her hand into the water. The surface shimmered and moved, lapping gently at her hand. The skin on her fingertips was twisted in a spiral shape like burn scars.

Boruto had seen that spiral shape before. He'd once read that this sort of scar came from the heat generated by electrical current passing through the body. It even had a name. "Lightning crest," he muttered.

Lily glanced his way before nodding slightly. "Yeah. You probably already guessed it, but my specialty is controlling other people with bioelectrical current. That's how I snuck out of house arrest, too. I got these crests during my training."

"Is the ability hereditary?" Boruto asked.

"It's learned." She pulled her hand from the water and waved it lightly, sending droplets scattering. "To acquire the technique, though, you need to practice actually sending current into a human being. Every single day, day after day, I fired electricity at my master. I was nine when I started training, and by the time I finally mastered it, I was fourteen."

"And your master?"

"My dad. The leader of Shigetsukyodan. My teacher." Even now, her very core grew dull and heavy when she remembered those days. It had been such extreme training.

Firing bolts of electricity at her own father had made little Lily cry. But her iron-fisted teacher had forced her to train, hitting her over and over until her tears stopped. He'd happily offered up his own body for the sake of his daughter's growth. For five years, she lived immersed in this daily hell. She was too inexperienced to properly control Lightning Style. She would sometimes even stop her teacher's heart with too strong a current. But even that pleased him.

You have a talent for Lightning Style. It is a gift from God so you can be of use to Shigetsukyodan. As he spoke, his face was free from care, even innocent. He had probably already been planning the attack on the neighboring Land of Fire.

Maybe he hasn't been in his right mind for a long time now, she thought. *Or maybe all that Lightning Style I poured into him made him lose his grip.*

"After I learned how to manipulate bioelectrical currents, it was decided that I would be sent to the village of Konohagakure. That was my break with my teacher. I insisted that the best strategy was for me to first make myself a part of the village and gain some position of influence, like as a manga artist or an actor or an idol. Once I had the ears of the people, I could teach them about Shigetsukyodan. But my master, he—" Her voice grew quieter. "He wasn't interested in spending any time on a real mission. He didn't want to send me to the Land of Fire as a missionary, as someone patiently building an audience and winning people over to our cause, but as a spy to inflict immediate damage. We argued about this over and over and over until finally…I fled the island alone."

"So you really did come to Konoha to become an idol?" Boruto asked. "Then that explosion on the Thunder Train…"

"They targeted the train because I was on it. With my master personally leading an elite squad. But that attack didn't end with my death, but my master's instead."

"He died?" Boruto furrowed his brow.

"When he was fighting your master, he got caught up in a comrade's technique," she told him.

Forced out of the carriage by a member of Shigetsukyodan, Lily had been rescued by Sasuke. Then she had seen the body skewered on the ceiling. The man pierced by the steel pillar, the man with the bib—Lily's master.

Lily's father.

"I knew they'd come for me again, so I figured I'd use that."

She shrugged. "And that's when I asked you to be my bodyguards."

"Because you thought we'd mess it up?" he asked.

"No. Because you're the Hokage's son."

A mix of emotions flitted across Boruto's face.

"I was going to take control of you and then show the audience you were a stand-in. The fans wouldn't be mad at me, the innocent idol, if the Hokage's son made a mess of my concert. I thought if I got the brunt of the outrage focused on a ninja protecting the village, it would do more to make the Land of Fire look bad than indiscriminately killing civilians, given that your country's supposed to be a symbol of prosperity and development."

"So that was your plan all along?" he asked.

"The concert was a failure, so I wanted to take you down this time for sure. I came after the ship, but I knew you'd scan the inside with the Sharingan first. So I glued myself to the hull for a while. Once I saw you all moving, I came inside."

"And then you controlled me again."

She shrugged.

Boruto let out a sigh and looked at her in exasperation as he grumbled, "Did you guys seriously think you could crush Konoha with such cowardly methods? If you've got the time and energy to attack others, use it to make your own island better."

"You're right." Lily lowered her eyes. "But, like, people are motivated by emotion, you know? I don't think I was right or anything. But the one thing I inherited from my master is a loyalty to my home. In the end, I couldn't walk away."

"Even when that master tried to kill you?" Boruto asked, incredulous.

"No." The strength drained out of her suddenly, and she leaned back against the wall. She felt like it was harder to breathe now, maybe because she had confessed her guilt. Even still, Lily continued to explain herself to Boruto as she took shallow breaths. "Education is important. We're basically monkeys when we're born. The fact that we're able to live rich, cultured lives is because we're educated. We're taught everything our ancestors learned before us. For better or for worse, we're slaves to the education we get from our parents and our society."

"Could you kill your comrades if your group told you to?" he asked.

"Of course," she replied without hesitation. "We think death is honorable. If you die fighting to spread the teachings of Shigetsukyodan, you go to heaven."

"I don't really get it." Boruto felt creeped out by Lily's words somehow. "But it's like… I dunno. Like, leaving your life or death to the group, it's just…not fair."

Not fair? Lily cocked her head curiously to one side.

Boruto continued falteringly, finding the subject almost too much for him. "I mean, ninja, we're changing with the times, too, y'know? My dad, the principal at the academy, everyone says so. Back in the old days, it would have been unthinkable to have a policy of capturing enemies instead of killing them whenever possible. But we live in an era of peace now, so we have the breathing room to do that kind of stuff. They say you gotta change with the times… Although all that stuff was before I was born, so I don't really know." Boruto lifted his face. The bright eyes he'd inherited from his father, eyes that were so much brighter than his father's, stared straight at Lily. "And then I guess what's left is a mix of the old stuff with the new stuff, adapted for us to use it now… I dunno."

"For me." Lily took a shallow breath. "I have such a hard time accepting that kind of thinking. I grew up having it beaten into me that our mission is to protect our doctrine, the religion that's been passed down for hundreds of years."

"I kinda get that, too," Boruto said slowly, staring at the dark water. "I used to totally hate science. I thought I'd never be okay with it. But Old Man Sasuke taught me all kinds of stuff, and it's like, I've started thinking that maybe it's not so bad as all that. Although there's still loads of stuff I can't accept. So…"

"What?" she challenged. "Are you trying to say you managed to change, so I can, too?"

"No, that's…not exactly it." Boruto fumbled for the words. He hated science. That feeling hadn't changed. But even so, maybe he had to start taking steps toward it. It was only since Sasuke became the master of Team Seven that he'd started thinking like this.

"We just had different educations, huh?" Lily said, sounding jealous somehow as she looked at Boruto. "I wanted to think freely the way you do. But it's too late now." She took a deep breath. "I can't change now. But yeah, the generation after me, I'm sure they'll adapt. I want to believe that."

Someone knocked on the roof.

"Boruto? You in there?" It was Mitsuki.

Boruto heaved a sigh of relief and sidled up to the ceiling. "Mitsuki! I'm here!"

"You sound okay. What about Lily?"

"I'm here," Lily said awkwardly.

"Thank goodness. Listen carefully, both of you." Mitsuki started speaking faster. "Sasuke froze the area around the ship with Ice Style so it wouldn't sink, but it looks like there's a big hole in the fuel tank. He says the oil might spill out into the ocean if we leave it like this."

"Seriously?!" Boruto yelled.

"And so, uh...the ship's going to fly in a minute. Can you fire your Rasengan straight down and escape once the ship's been in the air for ten seconds?"

Boruto and Lily exchanged a look, forgetting for a moment the situation they were in.

What? The boat's going to fly?

✖ ✖ ✖ ✖ ✖

"Amazing. It really is frozen." Sarada shivered at the cold air rising up around her. A massive lump of ice neatly surrounded the boat floating in the ocean. When she leaned forward and looked over the side of the boat, she had the strange sensation she was riding on top of a massive mountain of ice.

"Isn't salt water supposed to be hard to freeze?" she asked, looking back at her father on the deck.

"You know your stuff," Sasuke admired. "I didn't actually freeze the ocean water. First, I generated pure water with Water Style, and then I turned that water into ice."

"You changed the water to ice? How?"

He paused a moment. "It's a matter of imagination. The way water molecules move in relation to each other is what makes them water. And when the molecules are more tightly linked, they become ice." He turned the palm of his hand upward. Water began spilling out from between his fingers like a fountain. In an instant, it was frozen solid.

"Conversely, if the molecules separate from each other and start to move freely, that is steam." As if in response to his words, the frozen water melted, then evaporated, without leaving a single drop behind.

"It's gone," Sarada gasped.

"An application of Water Style," he told her. "A man I met once called Haku used changes in wind and water at the same time to generate ice. But that was a special technique, passed down within a single clan. Only they could master it. If you train, though, it's possible to do this much at least, even if you're not a member of the clan."

"I get it. That was actually pretty easy to understand, Dad, unlike your usual lessons," Sarada quipped.

Sasuke smiled slightly. "We should get started."

"Okay!" She ran to the prow of the ship where the massive anchor hung.

"Are you sure you can lift it?" *Don't push yourself,* he was about to say and then relaxed abruptly.

Sarada yanked the anchor up with both hands. "This is nothing."

"You take after your mother," he said.

Sarada turned a proud smile toward him. She hoisted the heavy anchor over her shoulder. The anchor was attached to the ship by a chain. The chain and its fastenings were frozen solid with Sasuke's Ice Style.

"Which way should I throw it, Dad?" she asked.

"Wherever you'd like. I'll follow your lead."

Feeling reassured, Sarada readjusted her grip on the anchor.

Lorentz Gun, tackled by father and daughter. But it wouldn't be a kunai that went flying. It would be the ship's anchor. They would make the anchor fly—dragging the whole ship along with it—before exploding the whole unit in midair to dispose of it. If they could burn it to ash with ultrahot flames, they could limit the damage to some ash on the ocean surface, which was far better than the oil leaking out into the water.

Sasuke looked back at the battered deck. Somewhere inside the frozen boat, there was a very stupid girl who had willingly jumped into the fissure in the deck and an idiot boy who'd gone after her without giving a thought to his own life. He had to save them and tell them not to be so reckless. It was his responsibility as Boruto's teacher.

Standing at the railing on the prow, Sarada lifted the anchor above her shoulders. "Here we go, Dad!"

"Anytime."

She sank down and took a deep breath before throwing the anchor as hard as she could. "Take that!" The steel anchor flew into the air, pulling the chain along with it.

From the palms of his open hands, Sasuke shot two crackling bolts of electricity.

The instant the electricity hit it, the anchor shot off faster than the human eye could follow. The chain snapped straight, and the block of ice around the boat began to creak and groan. A heartbeat later, the ice shattered, and the boat floated up. The sky grew larger before their eyes. Sarada staggered backwards. Sasuke caught her by the arm.

The massive ship slid along in the sky, yanked forward by the flying anchor.

✖ ✖ ✖ ✖ ✖

There was a sudden weightlessness that made Boruto's stomach rise up inside of him. A moment later, the force of gravity returned twice as strong.

Holding Lily with one hand and kneading his chakra with the other, Boruto counted. "Six...seven...eight..."

The ship began to creak and groan, unable to withstand its own weight and speed as it flew through the air. It was only a matter of time before it was yanked apart.

"Nine..."

Ten! Boruto turned his chakra into turbulent air and threw it down with his everything he had.

The roar of the lower half of the ship ripping away nearly shattered his eardrums. Lily might have been screaming beside him, but he couldn't hear anything. The shattered boat scattered to the wind. And then so did Boruto and Lily.

Far below them, he could see the dark ocean.

As they fell, Boruto scanned the water's surface. Off in the distance, there was something like an ice shelf, likely the flying ship's launch point. A narrow bridge of ice stretched out from the shelf, and on top of it, he could see Mitsuki casually waving to them with one hand. Next to him, the men in purple from the boat were tied together.

If he could avoid the frozen parts and use Wind Style to create a cushion before they hit the water, they should come out of this unscathed. The problem was that it wasn't just him; he had to keep Lily alive, too. He didn't know whether he could slow them down without ripping them apart. The odds were fifty-fifty.

"No other choice now." Boruto gritted his teeth. He was getting ready to try when flames suddenly exploded in the sky above them.

He looked in time to see the ship swallowed up by an explosion of such force it looked like it would reach the moon. The black flames would not go out until every last bit of the ship was consumed.

Sasuke's Inferno Style Flame Control.

Boruto didn't need anyone to tell him that the two shadows leaping from the burning boat were Sasuke and Sarada.

Sasuke held Sarada's arm as he chased after Boruto and Lily, adjusting the air resistance with his chakra. Once they were alongside Boruto, he tossed Sarada out and reached his hand out. "Boruto, give me Lily." He smiled at Boruto's hesitation. "Don't worry. I won't hurt her."

"Really?" Boruto asked.

"You don't trust your master?"

"That's no fair," he muttered and passed Lily to Sasuke. Perhaps from sheer terror, Lily had at some point lost consciousness.

"Dad! The water's coming up on us!" Sarada shouted.

To soften the impact of the water landing, all three ninja turned their Wind Style toward the ocean, the gusts pushing deep into the surface of the water.

There was a single large splash followed by two smaller ones. They all popped up to the surface again at the same time.

EPILOGUE

SASUKE'S STORY: STAR PUPIL

EPILOGUE

Boruto and his teammates looked up at the large screen hanging above the new town intersection.

"So Sasuke's decision to suspend the concert was the right one?"

"For the people of Konoha, yes. That extremist group was planning to bring their fight to the dome. I have no doubt that innocent people would have been killed if the show had continued."

"And you were once a member of this group, is that right, Lily?"

"I was. I disagreed with their methods, however, so I left. But I still held a grudge against the Hokage. I was determined to bring his standing down in the public eye."

"Was that why you became an idol then?"

"Yes. That's exactly right."

Himeno Lily was being interviewed. The fact that she had been allowed to do the live broadcast was quite extraordinary. Celebrity or not, she had committed a serious crime.

"Seriously, it totally sucks she turned out to be a criminal. I was halfway to being a fan even."

"Like, I knew Sasuke was a good guy right from the start. A hot old guy like that, there's no way he could be a baddie."

"Right? I mean, he's super cool, and so strong too!"

"I believe Lily, though. This is all a shinobi conspiracy!"

As he listened in on the people passing by him in the inter-section, Boruto grinned. Everyone had their own ideas about all the recent goings-on.

Lily herself had asked for the interview. She'd wanted to stand up in a public forum and tell people what had actually happened to clear away any misunderstandings.

The ninja had raised their eyebrows at the request. Who knew what would happen when the person at the center of the commotion stepped into the spotlight again? They would have a real problem on their hands if someone with as much influence as Lily were to say something extreme or careless on a live broadcast, and they were offended by the very notion of allowing a criminal to appear on TV. After careful deliberation, the council naturally rejected Lily's request, but in a surprise move, the Hokage overturned their decision and gave her per-mission to go ahead with the interview.

"Lily seems more relaxed now somehow," Sarada said.

"She kinda looks relieved," Boruto agreed.

Sitting on the sofa, Lily wore jeans and a simple, unbleached shirt rather than one of her usual frilly, ribbon-laden dresses. The hair on her head was her own close-cropped cut, which allowed a full view of the piercings in her ears. The overall effect was a neat chicness, an entirely different look from the idol Himeno Lily.

"That plan failed because the ninjas of Konoha interfered. Those same ninjas saved me when I tried to kill myself in a moment of despair. I asked for this interview because I wanted to express my gratitude to them. And because it seems that people have gotten the wrong idea about Sasuke, and I wanted to make clear what actually happened."

There was no mention of the fact that the ringleader behind

all of this had come out of the Shigetsukyodan. This too was the Hokage's work. He had no intention of rejecting the entire Shigetsukyodan community. He wanted to deepen their mutual solidarity. For the Shigetsukyodan followers to maintain their religion going forward, they would need to leave behind their exclusionary dogma and change to work with the outside world. The Hokage was hoping that Lily would help build that bridge. And her testimony had indeed been crucial in arresting the remainder of the extremist group.

"I guess the people of Shigetsu Island have accepted what happened surprisingly smoothly," Mitsuki said, looking up at the large screen. "This really was just the work of an out-of-control extremist group. It looks like not everyone in Shigetsukyodan hates the Land of Fire."

"I hope we can coexist somehow. Guess we just have to leave it to the Hokage and the Mizukage, huh?" Sarada said, and glanced at her watch. "Ah! Yikes! If we don't get going, Master Konohamaru'll get out before we get there!"

"Dang! We better hurry up!" Boruto shot off, and Sarada and Mitsuki chased after him.

✖ ✖ ✖ ✖ ✖

No longer in need of crutches, Konohamaru stood on his own feet and looked down at the courtyard from his window. Steam rose from the mug in his hand, black coffee he'd put more effort into brewing properly than usual. He celebrated his own complete recovery with the fragrant aroma of the freshly ground beans and the deep bitter taste. A gentle breeze came in through the window to caress his cheeks.

And then the whirlwind of his own beloved students blew in to shatter this silent, peaceful moment.

"Master Konohamaru! We came to visit!" Boruto shouted.

"You're too late, dummy," Konohamaru sighed. "I'm going home today." Brats. Noisy as ever. He looked back in exasperation and set his mug down on the side table.

"We know! That's why we came!" Sarada skipped into the room next, holding up a familiar paper bag and smiling. "We wanted you to have some strawberry daifuku this time for sure!"

"It's to celebrate your release," Mitsuki added, closing the door behind him.

The look on Konohamaru's face wavered faintly at the words *strawberry daifuku*.

"Th-that so? Well, you did come all the way here. Sit, stay awhile—hey."

They had already sat themselves down and were excitedly opening the box of daifuku, releasing the sweet, tart scent of the cakes into the room. Smiling faintly, Konohamaru watched his happy students distribute the confections. This time, he noticed, they'd only brought one for each of them.

"To your health!" Boruto grabbed a daifuku and stuffed it in his mouth.

As Konohamaru was reaching for the last daifuku in the box, there came a knock at the door.

"Come in!" Boruto called.

Sasuke entered. Konohamaru snapped to attention at the appearance of this unexpected visitor.

"I heard you were being released today," he said. "I came to check in on you before I set out."

"Thank you!" Konohamaru replied. "I'll be back at work tomorrow!"

"Oh?"

"Old Man Sasuke, you want a strawberry daifuku?!" Boruto immediately offered him the last cake, and Konohamaru very nearly screamed.

Boruto...That's my daifuku!

"No, I'll pass." Sasuke shook his head. "I don't care for sweets."

"Or natto," Sarada added.

"Oh yeah? Too bad. Okay then, I guess I'll eat it." The words had no sooner left his mouth than Boruto was tossing the daifuku into his mouth.

Konohamaru groaned. Boruto was already chewing, swallowing. *My strawberry daifuku…*

He only allowed himself to despair for an instant. When Uchiha Sasuke comes to visit, it is not time to fixate on daifuku. He quickly pulled himself together.

"You heading out again?" Boruto asked.

"Mm." Sasuke nodded. "This mission looks like it will go long."

"Be careful, okay, Dad?" Sarada said brightly and grabbed the edge of Sasuke's cloak. She was proud of her father and the way he kept the village safe, but her cheerfulness was half-faked.

She no longer felt anxious about her father's absences the way she used to as a child. She understood that the protection he offered them was the reason the village of Konoha was at last at peace. Even so, she couldn't help feeling sad about the fact that she couldn't be with her father, even if it was for the sake of his missions. She looked up at his expressionless face with envy.

I wish we could talk more when you actually are at home. Your face is always blank. I can't really tell if you're kind or not. Seriously, Dad. What are you thinking about all the time?

"Dad?"

"Hm?"

Overtaken by a sudden mischievous impulse, Sarada tugged on Sasuke's cloak. "You've got Mom's lipstick on your mouth."

After a brief silence, Sasuke rubbed his lips—which were entirely free of lipstick—still stony-faced. He seemed to have an inkling of how lipstick could have gotten there.

"I'm kidding. Mom doesn't even wear lipstick."

A trace of a grimace appeared on Sasuke's face as he lowered his arm. He was as strong as a demon in battle, and yet a little lie like this tripped him up. Sarada felt a surge of love for her father.

My dad's cooler than anyone else, but he's just a little bit cute, too.

"So, Dad, you actually really care about Mom, huh?"

"Sarada." Sasuke squatted down in front of her, looking slightly troubled, and poked her forehead with a finger. "We'll talk about that next time."

While he was at it, he also wiped away the daifuku filling sticking to the corners of her mouth. She grinned in delight and pressed a hand to her forehead.

"Ah!" Boruto peered into the box of daifuku and let out an anguished cry. "Ah, dangit! We only bought four today, so there's none left for Master Konohamaru!"

Konohamaru slumped as Boruto realized this bit of information too late. "Aah, it's fine." He waved a hand. "Don't worry about it. I've already given up on you kids ever letting me have one. I'll go buy some myself."

But Boruto leaped to his feet, practically knocking over the chair. "We'll go buy more!" he insisted. "If we line up now, we can still make it!"

"Whoa, whoa, simmer down. I'm fi—"

"It's okay. We haven't had our fill of them yet either!" Sarada said, and looked back at Mitsuki. "Let's go, Mitsuki!"

You're going to have more? These growing children seemed to have bottomless pits in the place of stomachs. Konohamaru rolled his eyes as his students trotted out of the hospital room. The two grown-ups were suddenly left alone, and the room fell silent.

Konohamaru sipped at his ice-cold coffee and looked at Sasuke with a wry smile. "They're a noisy bunch. Having them as students must have worn you out."

"No." Sasuke looked over at the door and a rare gentle

smile came across his face. "I had a fairly good time trying to pass on my own knowledge to the next generation. Although I don't know what they thought of the experience."

"You're too modest," Konohamaru insisted. "I'm sure it was the ultimate experience for them."

Sasuke's face abruptly softened. Strong like a demon, always cool and collected, the legendary ninja of the village of Konohagakure, Uchiha Sasuke. Konohamaru couldn't help but think perhaps, just maybe, he was the slightest bit mellower than he used to be.

"Sasuke. Take care on your next mission."

"Look after them," the other man replied, pulling his cloak around him. He started to walk out of the room and something slammed into him. When he lowered his gaze, he found Boruto standing before him. "What? Forget something?"

"Nah, I didn't forget a thing. I just... I wanted to say something." Boruto averted his eyes. It seemed that whatever he had to say, it wasn't easy for him to do it.

This boy was always cutting straight to the heart of things. What on earth could he be hesitating about now? Sasuke raised an eyebrow. "Does your stomach hurt?"

"Of course not! It's not that. Um..." Boruto took a deep breath and looked up at Sasuke. "So, okay, like...I still haven't learned enough from you, Old Man Sasuke. When you come back, I want you to be my teacher again!"

Sasuke widened his eyes, surprised by these unexpected words. He saw the features of his lifelong friend in the small face looking up at him. "Mm. I'll definitely be back. So you—"

"Of course! I'm totally gonna get strong! I'll be waiting for you!"

They met each other's eyes and grinned.

Sasuke was off to his new mission, Boruto to his days of

training. They would take all the things they'd gotten from each other to maintain peace in the village of Konohagakure in their own ways. With that shared devotion, whether they were near or far apart, the time would come when their paths would cross again, no doubt as master and student once more.

MASASHI KISHIMOTO

ABOUT THE CREATOR

Author/artist Masashi Kishimoto was born in 1974 in rural Okayama Prefecture, Japan. After spending time in art college, he won the Hop Step Award for new manga artists with his manga *Karakuri* (Mechanism). Kishimoto decided to base his next story on traditional Japanese culture. His first version of *Naruto*, drawn in 1997, was a one-shot story about fox spirits; his final version, which debuted in *Weekly Shonen Jump* in 1999, quickly became the most popular ninja manga in Japan.

JUN ESAKA

ABOUT THE AUTHOR

Born February 13 in Kanagawa Prefecture.
Blood type O. After graduating from
Waseda University, he began working as a writer.